INTRODUCTION TO FRENCH POETRY

A Dual-Language Book

EDITED BY
Stanley Appelbaum

DOVER PUBLICATIONS, INC.
New York

Copyright

Bibliographical Note

This Dover edition, first published in 1991, and reissued in 2004, is an unabridged and updated republication of the work originally published under the title *Invitation to French Poetry* by Dover Publications, Inc., New York, 1969.

This edition is also published together with a cassette (ISBN 0-486-99927-0) and a CD (0-486-99618-2), both under the title *Listen & Enjoy French Poetry.*

The following poems in this collection are reprinted by special permission: "Préface" by Paul Claudel; the selection from *Chronique* by Saint-John Perse; "Au premier mot limpide" and "Le Phénix" by Paul Éluard: all by permission of Editions Gallimard, Paris. "Les Lilas et les roses" by Aragon, by permission of the author. "Ici, toujours ici" and "Aube, fille des larmes, rétablis" by Yves Bonnefoy, by permission of Mercure de France, Paris. The French text of "L'Abeille" and "Le Vin perdu" by Paul Valéry, by permission of Éditions Gallimard. The authorized English translations of the works of Paul Valéry vest exclusively in Bollingen Foundation, New York. Their permission to publish the present translations [prepared specially for Dover] is gratefully acknowledged. The French text of "Les Colchiques" by Guillaume Apollinaire and of "Réveil" and "Dans la forêt sans heures" by Jules Supervielle, by permission of Éditions Gallimard. The English translations, prepared specially for Dover, are used by permission of New Directions Publishing Corporation, publishers of G. Apollinaire's and J. Supervielle's *Selected Writings.*

Library of Congress Cataloging-in-Publication Data

Invitation to French poetry.
    Introduction to French poetry / edited by Stanley Appelbaum. — Dover ed.
        p. cm. — (A Dual-language book)
    Previously published as: Invitation to French poetry.
    ISBN 0-486-26711-3
    1. French poetry—Translations into English. 2. English poetry—Translations from French. 3. French poetry—History and criticism. 4. Poets, French—Biography. 5. French poetry. I. Appelbaum, Stanley. II. Title. III. Series.

PQ1170.E6158 1991
841.008—dc20

                    90-23240
                    CIP

Manufactured in the United States of America
Dover Publications, Inc., 31 East 2nd Street, Mineola, N.Y. 11501

CONTENTS

CONTENTS

INTRODUCTION

I

THE conquests of French prose, both as an international medium of cultural communication and as an incredibly supple vehicle for the thoughts of the great French essayists and novelists, have been so outstanding that even in their homeland the achievements of the French poets—aside from a few magical names in the Symbolist and Surrealist generations—are often neglected. Such neglect is unjust. The French poetic heritage is one of great richness and can boast of many unique contributions to world literature. Moreover, in the thirteenth century, in the crucial sixteenth, in the nineteenth and twentieth, the influence of French poets on their counterparts in England (not to mention other nations of the Continent and the Americas) has been decisive.

As in many other countries, so too in France the earliest literary monuments are in poetic form, a form that already testifies to a long, now-silent evolution. Several verse biographies of saints date from the eleventh century. The distinguished series of epic *chansons de geste* (the most famous being the *Chanson de Roland*) begin early in the twelfth century, about the same time as the first narrative poems based on figures and events of ancient history. Chrestien de Troyes and Marie de France introduce themes from Celtic legend in the second half of the twelfth century, which also witnesses the rise of the short lyric: dance poems, "romances" (in the Iberian sense) and a wealth of forms, simple or subtle, inspired by the Provençal poets.

The thirteenth century sees the flowering of the medieval lyric, poems of love and good cheer, of politics and religion, in a variety of forms not matched again until the nineteenth century; alongside scores of anonymous pieces we find works by such vibrant personalities as the *jongleurs* Colin Muset and Rutebeuf. This is also the century of the *fabliaux*, of charming verse plays, of didactic works, of the much-imitated *Roman de Renart* animal "epics" and of that most influential of all allegories, the *Roman de la Rose*, begun by Guillaume de Lorris and completed some fifty years after his death by Jean de Meung.

In the greatly troubled fourteenth century many old forms live on with diminished vigor; the lyric becomes increasingly formalized—with great emphasis on such types as the *rondeau*, *virelai* and *ballade*—in the works of Guillaume de Machaut (*c.* 1300–1377) and Eustache Deschamps (*c.* 1346–*c.* 1406).

By the fifteenth century, at which point this anthology begins, French poetry has already been endowed with the verse forms which will chiefly characterize it henceforth, the decasyllable, the octosyllable and the famous alexandrine; with several stanza complexes (such as the *ballade*) which will be used for centuries to come; and with a splendid tradition of themes, "mythologies" and attitudes. The fifteenth-century poets represented here, CHARLES D'ORLÉANS and VILLON, are perfecters, not inventors, of form, however much they enrich the emotive content of French poetry. It is interesting to note how this prince and this hungry highwayman, meeting at the close of the Middle Ages, symbolize the incomparable range in social and economic status of the poets of this exciting period.

Faithful to aging medieval fancies but already touched by Italian humanism, CLÉMENT MAROT is a pivotal figure in the first part of the great Renaissance century. This sixteenth century was to be one in which many poets would enjoy vast personal prestige but would be largely dependent on the patronage of kings and nobles. Exceptional in this respect are the bourgeois poets of the Lyons group (about 1540 to 1560), strongly moved by the forms (especially the sonnet) and themes (especially Petrarchism and Platonism) of their Italian contemporaries; the chief Lyons poets are MAURICE SCÈVE and LOUISE LABÉ.

The influence of the newly rediscovered Greek writers, reaction against the preponderant use of Latin in "serious" literature in

France, and the impatient stirrings of fresh young talents: these are the main ingredients of the mid-sixteenth-century poetic revolution of the *Pléiade*, which introduced the ode and several other forms into French and affected poetic vocabulary profoundly. The history of French literature is punctuated with many a "school" like the *Pléiade* and many a manifesto like the 1549 *Deffence et Illustration*, but all the truly important "schools" have really been loosely knit groups of friends or like-minded poets, of whom the most gifted have generally produced their best poems while working out their personal poetic destinies. No other poets of the *Pléiade* can compete with RONSARD or DU BELLAY, although Jean Antoine de Baïf (1532–1589) and Remy Belleau (1528–1577), to name just two others, deserve attention. Among the many worthy post-*Pléiade* poets, Théodore Agrippa d'Aubigné (1552–1630) is preeminent for his long and impassioned pro-Huguenot work *Les Tragiques*.

The sixteenth century, one of enormous vitality, was also characterized by tireless experiments with poetic form. Those innovations based on Greek and Latin syllabic quantity, though instructive, were doomed to failure; those involving rhythmic prose or the suppression of rhyme were to have belated echoes in the nineteenth century; those based on contemporary Italian practice were to enjoy tremendous success: not only the sonnet, perfected by the *Pléiade* and still very much with us, but also the *stances*, poems made up of equal short stanzas, first imported late in the sixteenth century and of great significance in the seventeenth.

The seventeenth century opens powerfully with the reforms of MALHERBE, who by his restrictive but well-planned regulation of rhythm and vocabulary and his condemnation of the assertive figure or image, may be said to have established the tone of "noble" poetry for the next two hundred years and more. The satirist Mathurin Régnier (1573–1613), a chief source of Molière's prosody and subject matter, was more a personal than a doctrinal opponent of Malherbe; nevertheless he represents in this period the important elements of thematic freedom and colloquial diction in French poetic history. In fact, as pleasant as the works may be of Malherbe's two chief disciples, François

3

Maynard (1582–1646) and Racan (Honorat de Bueil, seigneur de Racan, 1589–1670), the most delightful poets of the first half of the century are three whose reckless spirits or adventurous lives, in conjunction with their more unconventional sensibilities (especially a warm feeling for nature), made them impatient of the Malherbian ethos: Théophile de Viau (1590–1626), Tristan L'Hermite (c. 1601–1655) and the protean SAINT-AMANT. Religious poetry, like that of the dramatist Pierre Corneille (1606–1684), is important in this part of the century. The literary epic is also widely practiced, with little success. An essential feature of the period is the importance of female patrons in literary circles. The finest purveyor of light verse for the salons of the *précieuses* is Vincent Voiture (1598–1648).

The reign of Louis XIV (especially from 1660 to 1700) is often considered the golden, or Classical, era of French literature. The four most eminent representatives of poetry in this period are Jean Racine (1639–1699), whose tragedies and biblical dramas (in alexandrine couplets) contain probably the suavest, most nearly perfect verse in the French language; Molière (Jean-Baptiste Poquelin, 1622–1673), whose inventive characterizations outshine poetic form in those of his comedies which employ verse; the highly influential critic and satirist Nicolas Boileau-Despréaux (1636–1711); and that amalgam of Gallic verve and ageless grace, LA FONTAINE, who sums up as well as any one man could the diverse tendencies of his century.

As in the seventeenth, so in the eighteenth century up to the 1789 Revolution, patronage remains important, but the increasing independence of the bourgeoisie even in the arts is exemplified by the phenomenal career of VOLTAIRE. Better known for his prose works, Voltaire nevertheless is the paramount poet of the first two thirds of the century, matching the pompousness of such ode writers as Jean Baptiste Rousseau (1670–1741) and the playfulness of the flocks of "Marotic" epigrammatists, while excelling in the philosophic poem as then practiced. It is often said that France had no poetry during this period, but this is an exaggeration—there is more than one kind of poetry. What *is* sadly lacking is the poem that seeks to cast a spell by its "pictorial" or "musical" powers.

Things improve in the last third of the century, which ushers in the reign of sentiment that creates the atmosphere for the Romantic movement. Along with the nature studies of Jean François Saint-Lambert (1716–1803) and Jean-Antoine Roucher (1745–1794) we encounter the personal sorrow of Nicolas-Joseph Gilbert (1751–1780) and the exotically tinged love lyrics of two poets born (like Leconte de Lisle) on the island of Réunion: Antoine de Bertin (1752–1790) and Évariste Parny (1753–1814). The work of ANDRÉ CHÉNIER (almost none of which was published during his lifetime) is the crowning achievement of this period. Yet there is no doubt that during this largely "rational" century, dominated by the essay and thesis-fiction, and then during the oppressive years of the Revolution and the Empire, the prestige of poetry declines sharply.

All the more striking, then, is the self-glorifying upsurge of Romanticism contemporary with the Restoration. Often considered the last decisive turning point in the history of French literature to date, the Romantic movement—rediscovering vivid aspects of the Middle Ages and the Renaissance, turning its eyes toward Spain and the Orient, assimilating recent trends of English and German literature—restores emotion and enchantment to French poetry and at the same time adds new life and flexibility to technical aspects of versification that had become hardened since Malherbe's reforms. This is an era of mighty personalities, and the individual biographies of a LAMARTINE, a VIGNY, a HUGO or a MUSSET are far more meaningful than arbitrary group studies. The nineteenth century also establishes the modern pattern of the poet's economic status: most of the poets are now professional writers who, when not attracted to a Bohemian existence, generally have to support themselves with other types of work, very often journalism.

The first half of the century abounds in interesting figures, who cannot all be mentioned; one of the most fascinating is France's greatest popular poet, Pierre Jean de Béranger (1780–1857).

At mid-century the paths diverge. There is the lonely but prophetic road of GÉRARD DE NERVAL. There is the unemotional "art for art's sake" approach of GAUTIER, which will inspire the Parnassians. There is the subtle alchemy of BAUDELAIRE, whose meticulous craftsmanship will also provide a model for the Parnassians, but whose greatest contributions are the use of imagery and verbal music that links him to the Symbolists, and the total commitment of his life to poetry that makes him the spiritual progenitor of the many great figures since his day who have sought for salvation through their art.

The second half of the century is a time of great fulfillment and promises for the future. Each in his own way—MALLARMÉ, the constructor of hermetic microcosms; VERLAINE the self-tormentor; and RIMBAUD, the footloose rebel—reinterpret the lessons of Baudelaire. The poets grouped about Mallarmé call themselves the Symbolists. Those who attach themselves to Verlaine at a certain moment become known as the Decadents. The Parnassians (named for their participation in the anthology *Le Parnasse contemporain*, 1866, 1871 and 1876) are represented chiefly by the learned and haughty bard of the aridity of existence, Charles-Marie-René Leconte de Lisle (1818–1894), and by the Cuban-born sonneteer José Maria de Heredia (1842–1905). There is no dearth of other confraternities.

The most fascinating of the poets who remain aloof from these "schools" and "chapels" are three ingenious if imperfect writers who all died at an early age: the sea-haunted Tristan Corbière (1845–1875) and the two Montevideans, Isidore Ducasse (the "Comte de Lautréamont," 1847–1870), author of the startlingly fierce *Chants de Maldoror*, and Jules Laforgue (1860–1887), whose sad, off-key humor was to influence Apollinaire and many others in France and elsewhere.

A special topic within a survey of nineteenth-century poetry is the rise of the prose poem. Practiced with success in the first half of the century by Aloysius (or Louis) Bertrand (1807–1841), author of *Gaspard de la nuit*, and Maurice de Guérin (1810–1839), it was more fully exploited by Baudelaire and perfected by Rimbaud, who is the real inspirer of the innumerable poets who have since used this flexible form. The late nineteenth-century writers, partially influenced by Walt Whitman, also investigated many aspects of blank verse and free verse.

Among the poets who had reached maturity by 1900, those who most nearly dominated the next half-century by their example were CLAUDEL and VALÉRY—Claudel, the fervent Catholic, of boundless imagination and fluid, seething form, and Valéry, the humanist and skeptic, suspicious of inspiration and a fastidious tyrant over words.

APOLLINAIRE is largely a poet of transition, a torchbearer between certain "underground" trends of the late nineteenth century and more radical departures of the twentieth. The great poetic adventure of this century, which Apollinaire dubbed before it existed, was that of Surrealism. After the post-World War I avant-garde terrain had been cleared by the shock troops of Dada, among whom André Breton (1896–1966), ARAGON and ÉLUARD did valiant service, these three joined forces in the more constructive Surrealist movement. The political and social plans of the movement may have misfired, but its influence on literature and the figurative arts throughout the world could hardly have been more profound. In the field of poetry Surrealism exploited the subconscious and the world of dreams, aiming at "illogical" but arresting reassemblages of figures and images. Éluard, Aragon and several other important poets were later to depart from the Surrealist fold, Breton remaining as guardian of its orthodoxy. His death in 1966 deprived Surrealism of its devoted leader. Meanwhile, SUPERVIELLE and SAINT-JOHN PERSE created major poetic languages of their own.

Among poets born since World War I, the reputation of YVES BONNEFOY is perhaps the most securely established.

Other fine modern poets whose work would surely have been represented here had space permitted include Charles Péguy (1873–1914), who wrote compelling religious poetry strongly tinged with national pride; Pierre Reverdy (1889–1960), whose free-verse reorganization of sensory data influenced the Surrealists, but whose discreet music is all his own; Pierre Jean Jouve (1887–1976), whose poetry of anguished dismemberment between Christ and the flesh often reaches white heat; and René Char (1907–1988), whose courageous acceptance of earthly life is expressed in stripped, granite-like poems quite unusual in French.

The twentieth century has also witnessed the development of a more original and vital French-language poetry in many countries

7

that were once French colonies or protectorates. The French-speaking African nations are now in the forefront of this trend, and no serious survey of current French poetry can be complete that does not take into account the work of writers like the Senegalese Léopold Sédar Senghor (born 1906).

II

A reference, however brief, to the formal aspects of versification cannot well be omitted in an introduction to French poetry, since the metrical patterns established in the Middle Ages have retained their power throughout its history and still echo in the work of present-day poets, who may adhere to them strictly, vary them subtly or allude to them fleetingly, but can rarely ignore them if their work is at all metrical.

In its more orthodox form, the French verse, or single line of poetry, lives by a tension between a fixed number of syllables, theoretically of equal weight, and the ever-varying rhythms imposed by the expressive content of the words. In counting syllables it must be remembered that mute *e*'s at the end of words are elided before following vowels or mute *h*'s, and that in so-called feminine verses the very last syllable (always ending in -*e*, -*es* or the -*ent* of third-person verb endings) is not included in the count. Thus, a typical octosyllabic verse in Valéry's "Le Vin perdu" (p. 142):

Sa transparence accoutumée

is scanned:

1   2   3   4   5   6   7   8
Sa trans-pa-rencᴇ ac-cou-tu-mé-ᵉ

Here we can do no more than trace rapidly some of the vicissitudes of the best-known meter in French poetry, the alexandrine. Although its name is derived from its use in numerous narrative poems about Alexander the Great written around the turn of the thirteenth century, this meter was employed much more widely throughout the Middle Ages, even figuring in lyric stanzas. Its earliest extant appearance is in the brief and rather primitive epic *Le Pèlerinage de Charlemagne* (The Pilgrimage of Charlemagne, about 1150), where it already displays its characteristic elements—twelve syllables, with a discernible pause (caesura) after the sixth

8

—and is already handled with a degree of skill and taste:

L'emperedre descent dessour lo marbre blanc

| 1 | 2 | 3 | 4 | 5 | 6 | | 7 | 8 | 9 | 10 | 11 | 12 |

L'em-pe-re-dre de-scent | de-ssour lo mar-bre blanc

(The Emperor descends onto the white marble)

The sixteenth century was vital in the history of the alexandrine, the Lyons group, the *Pléiade* and such poets as d'Aubigné making use of it in sonnets, didactic poems and many other works, and constantly refining it and exploiting its technical possibilities.

The firm and rhythmic alexandrine of the seventeenth century, in which it was desirable for the syntactic thought to be complete within the single verse (somewhat as in Marlowe's "mighty line"), is largely a gift of Malherbe (p. 52):

N'esperons plus, mon ame, aux promesses du monde

In the Golden Age of Louis XIV we find the marvelously poised alexandrine of Racine (quoted from *Phèdre*, Act IV, Scene 6):

Ah! combien frémira son ombre épouvantée
(Ah! how his ghostly shade will tremble in its fright)

alongside the relaxed, conversational and often mischievous alexandrine of La Fontaine's *Fables* (p. 62):

Tout le jour, il avoit l'œil au guet; et la nuit

In this example note the incompleteness of the syntax at the end and the relative weakness of the caesura between "avoit" and "l'œil" (the normal reading or reciting tendency being to group these words within one breath).

Nothing new occurs until the work of André Chénier, who enriches the fading alexandrine of the eighteenth century musically and often employs bolder *enjambement* (running on of syntax to a new line).

The Romantic and post-Romantic poets of the nineteenth century. whose revolution in mood and subject matter is great, make certain quite tangible changes in the alexandrine, but do

9

not really alter the nature of this strongly traditional meter. We encounter very striking *enjambement* (Mallarmé, p. 118):

> Rêvant, l'archet aux doigts, dans le calme des fleurs
> Vaporeuses, . . .

heady musical effects (Baudelaire, p. 112):

> Les houles, en roulant les images des cieux

and new subdivisions of the line in which the standard bisecting caesura disappears (Hugo, p. 92):

> Seul, inconnu, le dos courbé, les mains croisées

Seul, in-con-nu, le dos (¦) cour-bé, les mains croi-sé-ées

Some alexandrines of the second half of the century even have a single polysyllabic word straddling the caesura, while others can hardly be scanned except as whole blocks of twelve syllables.

The twentieth century, has, of course, been very free in its treatment of versification, but the (relatively) "standard" alexandrine is still widely used exactly as bequeathed by the nineteenth century or with slight variations. One very common variation is the well-calculated placement here and there of an additional syllable, most often one ending in a discreet mute *e* (first example, Apollinaire, p. 148; second example, Éluard, p. 164):

> Les enfants de l'école viennent avec fracas

> Foyer de terre foyer d'odeurs et de rosée

Moreover, the alexandrine can often be found embedded within such modern configurations as the *"verset"* of Claudel (p. 136):

> Donne avec un profond ¦ tressaillement, mon âme, dans ce
> pays complètement inconnu!

in the very long lines of Saint-John Perse (p. 160):

> Pour nous chante déjà ¦ plus hautaine aventure. Route
> frayée (etc.)

and even in free verse like Breton's.

This hallowed meter, along with the decasyllable and octosyllable, would still appear to have a long future in French poetry.

III

It is hoped that, within its obvious limitations, this anthology will be found representative of the main tendencies in French poetic history and will at the same time offer a glimpse of the great variety of this important cultural legacy.

Since I was interested only in original texts and not in "modernizations" that of necessity are really translations into current French, I have most regretfully omitted all but the last stages of medieval production: even those medieval dialects which contributed most heavily toward the formation of modern standard French are too different from it to be readily accessible to beginning students or the general reader, while many of the most famous poems of the Middle Ages were composed in much less familiar dialects.

Emphasis has been placed on lyric poetry and poems that are related to the lyric even though of satirical or epic aspect. Verse drama, being truly different in nature, was categorically excluded; no one can lament the absence of Racine more than I.

An important aim has been to include only complete pieces, even though several major poets, especially of the early Romantic generations (Hugo, Musset), were at their best in works too extended for an anthology of this size. Lamartine and Vigny had to be represented by excerpts if they were to be included at all.

Naturally, I urge the reader to make good all these deficiencies on his own as soon as he is able.

The texts of the poems included here have been reprinted from the best critical editions available to me, or, for the most recent pieces, from the definitive versions approved by the poets. After long and serious reflection, I have printed the fifteenth- through seventeenth-century texts with their orthography unretouched. Although some readers may be momentarily disconcerted by the older spellings or even taken aback at apparently "wrong" or "missing" accents, I am confident that upon greater familiarity with the poems they will prize the authenticity of this presentation.

The new English translations in this volume, which follow the French text line for line in so far as the differences between the two languages permit, are definitely not intended to be poetic re-creations of the original works, but merely aids to the understanding of the content. The translations aim to be as literal as possible, but without doing violence to idiomatic English expression or emulating the lifeless productions of a "pony" or a computer.

The portraits of poets reproduced here are authentic; to the best of my knowledge, there are no "artist's conceptions." For the poets who lived before the age of photography, original versions of their portraits have been sought, and copies and redrawings rejected, as far as possible. There is no known portrait of either Villon or Saint-Amant; other illustrative material has been used in these cases.

In the preparation of the brief biographies and analyses of the poets, every attempt has been made to sift the latest information available on the subject. In recent years, particularly in France itself, a host of devoted scholars—who are too numerous to mention here, but to all of whom, without singling out any, I would now like to express my appreciation—have been extremely active in throwing light on the lives of less well known poets and clarifying details in the lives of even the most famous. To give only one instance: almost unbelievably, there was no truly critical biography of a poet as important as Saint-Amant until 1964. This recent scholarship has largely taken the form of salutary destruction of time-honored myths concerning many figures, so that new brief biographical sketches like the ones in *Introduction to French Poetry* are sometimes likely to be more striking for what they omit than for what they include.

The dates assigned here to poems and other works are those of their first publication in book form unless otherwise stated. The translations of book and poem titles are literal, and may not always coincide with those of published English translations of the works.

It is the sincere wish of anthologist and publisher that the present collection will encourage the reader to extend his acquaintance with this fascinating area of literature.

Le temps a laisse son manteau
De vent de froidure et de pluye
Et sest vestu de brouderie
De soleil luyant cler et beau
Il nya beste ne oyseau
Quen son jargon ne chante ou cue
Le temps &c.
Riviere fontaine et ruisseau
Portent en livree iolie
Gouttes dargent dorfaverie
Chascun sabille de nouueau
Le temps &c.

CHARLES D'ORLÉANS

Born in Paris, 1394; died at Amboise, 1465

CHARLES DE VALOIS was already addicted to poetry when, at fourteen, he became Duke of Orleans after the murder of his father (Louis d'Orléans, brother of the French king Charles VI) by assassins in the pay of the Duke of Burgundy. It was several years before Charles could patch up a truce with Burgundy and restore the wavering reputation of his household. In 1408 he married Isabelle of France, widow of the English king Richard II; she died the next year. The continued enmity of the Burgundians (inflamed by Charles's second political marriage, 1410, to Bonne d'Armagnac, who died about 1435) brought the English into France and led to Charles's capture at Agincourt in 1415. He spent the next twenty-five years as a political prisoner in various parts of England.

During his seldom rigorous captivity, Charles learned English thoroughly and celebrated, with great felicity in two languages, his love for two English noblewomen. It was during this period that he composed not only all his English poetry but also most of his French *ballades* and *chansons*. Hardly any of the feverish political and military agitation of these years, which saw the entire public career of Joan of Arc, is reflected in the poems.

Returning to France in 1440, Charles spent nearly a decade in a flurry of diplomatic activity leading to a truce with England, and in a hapless invasion of Piedmont, then retired to his château at Blois, where he held a poetic court that extended hospitality to all men of talent, from royal scions like René of Anjou to starveling criminals like Villon. In this period he wrote most of his *rondeaux*, traditional short fixed-form lyrics with recurring lines. One example (number 31) is presented here.

15

One of the three children of Charles's declining years born to his third wife, Marie of Clèves, became Louis XII of France.

The poetry of Charles d'Orléans is unmatched in French for its combination of ease, grace and musicality with a glittering perfection of form that recalls the "goldsmith's work" he speaks of in his famous spring *rondeau*. The personified allegorical figures (Youth, Hope, Melancholy and many others) which he inherited

"*Le temps a laissié son manteau*"

Le temps a laissié son manteau
De vent, de froidure et de pluye,
Et s'est vestu de brouderie,
De soleil luyant, cler et beau.

Il n'y a beste, ne oyseau,
Qu'en son jargon ne chante ou crie:
Le temps a laissié son manteau!

Riviere, fontaine et ruisseau
Portent, en livree jolie,
Gouttes d'argent d'orfaverie,
Chascun s'abille de nouveau:
Le temps a laissié son manteau.

from the *Roman de la Rose* tradition become in his hands charming maskers who join the poet in his subtle autobiographical studies of the ravages of age and of his lonely withdrawal into the apathetic resignation of *Nonchaloir*. His verses, with their countless allusions to music, chess, law, hunting, medicine, Valentine's and May Day customs, are a verbal counterpart to the exquisite contemporary miniatures of the Books of Hours.

"The season has shed its mantle"

The season has shed its mantle
Of wind, cold and rain,
And has clothed itself in embroidery,
In gleaming sunshine, bright and fair.

There is no animal or bird
That does not sing or call in its own tongue:
The season has shed its mantle!

Stream, fountain and brook
Bear, as handsome livery,
Silver drops of goldsmith's work;
Everyone puts on new garments:
The season has shed its mantle.

Epitaphe dudit villon

Freres humains qui apres no⁹ vives
Nayez les cueurs contre no⁹ endurcis
Car se pitie de no⁹ pouurez auez
Dieu en aura pluftoft de vous mercis
Vous nous voies cy ataches cinq fix
Quãt de la char q̃ trop auõs nourrie
Elleft pieca deuouree et pourrie
et no⁹ les os deuends cẽdres τ pouldre
De noftre mal personne ne sen rie
Mais pries dieu que tous nous veuil
le absouldre   g iii.

FRANÇOIS VILLON

Born in Paris, c. 1431

VILLON is the first French writer who reveals himself to us as a complete and unique human being, with all his faults upon his head. Displaying thorough mastery of traditional poetic techniques, he enlivens the medieval forms and fancies with vivid personal observation drawn from his unsavory but intense existence.

Born François de Montcorbier (or des Loges), the poet adopted the surname of the pious Guillaume Villon, who cared for him in childhood. François's exuberant university life (he became a Master of Arts in 1452) was interrupted temporarily in 1455 after he killed a rowdy priest in a brawl, and permanently at the end of 1456, when he fled Paris after stealing a large sum from the treasury of the Faculty of Theology. Just about this time Villon wrote a brief mock will in verse, the lighthearted *Lais* (Legacies, also called *Le petit Testament*).

There followed years of footloose wandering throughout France, during which Villon briefly visited the poetic courts of Charles d'Orléans at Blois and Jean II, Duke of Bourbon, at Moulins. Villon's poems in thieves' jargon and several other short pieces date from this period. In 1461 he was imprisoned at Meung-sur-Loire and was released only when the new king, Louis XI, passed through the town dispensing amnesties.

Returning to the outskirts of Paris, Villon composed his longest work, probably early in 1462. This was *Le Testament* (also called *Le grand Testament*), another humorous will, but one filled with more serious overtones and haunted by the specter of death. In this *Testament* Villon inserted several lyric poems that rank among his best work, especially the "Ballade des dames du temps jadis"

19

(Ballad of the Ladies of the Past), with its refrain, "Mais où sont les neiges d'antan?" (But where are the snows of yesteryear?).

At the end of 1462 Villon was again in prison, this time sentenced to be hanged. It was then that he wrote his "Épitaphe" or "Ballade des pendus" (Ballad of the Hanged Men), included here; the poet sees himself as already executed and begs the indulgence of his fellow men. In January 1463 his sentence was commuted to exile far from Paris; after this point the course of his life is completely unknown.

Villon is not only the poet par excellence of the storms of young blood, but also the first of many great chroniclers of Parisian life,

L'Épitaphe

Freres humains, qui après nous vivez,
N'ayez les cuers contre nous endurcis,
Car, se pitié de nous povres avez,
Dieu en aura plus tost de vous mercis.
Vous nous voiez cy attachez cinq, six:
Quant de la chair, que trop avons nourrie,
Elle est pieça devorée et pourrie,
Et nous, les os, devenons cendre et pouldre.
De nostre mal personne ne s'en rie,
Mais priez Dieu que tous nous vueille absouldre!

Se freres vous clamons, pas n'en devez
Avoir desdaing, quoy que fusmes occis
Par justice. Toutesfois, vous sçavez
Que tous hommes n'ont pas bon sens assis;
Excusez nous—puis que sommes transsis—
Envers le filz de la Vierge Marie,
Que sa grace ne soit pour nous tarie,
Nous preservant de l'infernale fouldre.
Nous sommes mors, ame ne nous harie;
Mais priez Dieu que tous nous vueille absouldre!

especially in its intimate and clandestine aspects. Nevertheless, he is also capable of sincere religious feeling, as in the "Ballade des pendus."

The complicated medieval *ballade* form was possibly never more brilliantly handled than in this "Épitaphe." As shown here it includes three stanzas (each consisting of ten lines with ten syllables each) and a brief *envoi*, all using the same rhymes; each stanza ends with the same line. Here, however, technical wizardry is overshadowed by the poem's genuine emotion and startling immediacy of vision.

Epitaph

Men, our brothers, who live after us,
Do not harden your hearts against us,
For if you take pity on us poor wretches,
God will be more readily merciful toward you.
You see five or six of us hanging here:
As for our flesh, which we nourished all too well,
It has long since been devoured or has rotted,
And we, the bones, are becoming ashes and dust.
Let no one laugh at our misfortune,
But pray God that He may absolve all of us!

If we call you brothers, you should not
Be contemptuous, even though we were executed
By the law. Still you know
That not all men have firm common sense;
Intercede for us—now that we are no more—
With the Son of the Virgin Mary,
That His grace may not run dry for us,
But may save us from the lightning of Hell.
We are dead, let no soul trouble us;
But pray God that He may absolve all of us!

La pluye nous a buez et lavez,
Et le soleil desechez et noircis;
Pies, corbeaulx, nous ont les yeux cavez,
Et arraché la barbe et les sourcilz.
Jamais, nul temps, nous ne sommes assis;
Puis ça, puis la, comme le vent varie,
A son plaisir sans cesse nous charie,
Plus becquetez d'oiseaulx que dez à couldre.
Ne soiez donc de nostre confrairie,
Mais priez Dieu que tous nous vueille absouldre!

ENVOI

Prince Jhesus, qui sur tous a maistrie,
Garde qu'Enfer n'ait de nous seigneurie:
A lui n'ayons que faire ne que souldre.
Hommes, icy n'a point de mocquerie,
Mais priez Dieu que tous nous vueille absouldre!

The rain has steamed and washed us,
And the sun has dried and blackened us;
Magpies, crows, have gouged out our eyes,
And pulled out our beards and eyebrows.
Never at any time are we at rest;
Now here, now there, as the wind changes,
It moves us unceasingly at its pleasure;
The birds have pecked us more full of holes than a thimble.
Thus do not be of our brotherhood,
But pray God that He may absolve all of us!

ENVOI

May Prince Jesus, Who is the master over all,
Keep Hell from having lordship over us:
Let us have nothing to do with and nothing to pay to Hell.
Men, there is no raillery here,
But pray God that He may absolve all of us!

CLÉMENT MAROT

Born in Cahors, 1496; *died in Turin, 1544*

CLÉMENT MAROT, born in the Southwest of France, in-
herited from his father Jean not only the post of secretary
to François I, but also the playful techniques and late Gothic
stereotypes of the poetic generation of the "*Grands Rhétoriqueurs.*"
Nevertheless, Clément has multiple claims to fame as an inno-
vator: as the first French sonneteer (he became acquainted with
the form, and with Italian humanism in general, during his first
exile), as the winner of the first publicized satiric debate in France
(in which Marot defended the new "natural" style against the
poetaster Sagon), and as an experimenter with numerous forms
and themes that clearly influenced the *Pléiade* poets, La Fontaine
and many others. Yet Marot is best known and loved for his
distinctly personal contributions to French poetry: abounding
wit, coupled with that delight in spicy entertainments known to
the French as *gauloiserie* (this trait, together with an artificial
archaism of language not typical of Marot, was to characterize
the so-called *style marotique* of the seventeenth and eighteenth
centuries). No less genuine a component of Marot's complex
nature was his strong leaning toward the religious ideals of the
Reformation, a loyalty which caused him much suffering in that
era of vicious persecutions.

Jailed for a short period in 1526 and again in 1532 for eating
bacon publicly during Lent, Marot finally decided in 1534 that
France was temporarily too dangerous for him. After spending
about a year in Ferrara, from which city he launched the notorious

* At least one Marot scholar has decided on the basis of varied evi-
dence that the poet was born not less than ten years earlier, but this
seems to create serious problems of chronology.

poetic competition of the *Blasons du corps féminin* (glorifications of all parts of the female anatomy), and some time in Venice, he returned home in 1536, making a solemn recantation of his "errors." But the publication of his translations of thirty Psalms (in short strophes meant to be set to music), and of an earlier work, *L'Enfer* (Hell), denouncing magistrates, led to a new, final exile. In Calvin's Geneva he brought the number of his Psalm translations up to fifty; this work quickly became the standard Huguenot songbook. But his libertine attitudes soon made him *persona non grata* in Geneva, and he kept moving on until he died in Turin in September 1544.

De la jeune Dame qui a vieil mary

En languissant, et en grefve tristesse
Vit mon las cueur, jadis plein de liesse,
Puis que lon m'a donné Mary vieillard.
Helas pourquoy? rien ne sçait du vieil art
Qu'apprend Venus, l'amoureuse Deesse.

    Par un desir de monstrer ma prouesse
Souvent l'assaulx: mais il demande: où est ce?
Ou dort, peult estre, et mon cueur veille à part
      En languissant.

    Puis quand je veulx luy jouer de finesse,
Honte me dict: Cesse, ma fille, Cesse!
Garde t'en bien, à honneur prens esgard!
Lors je respons: Honte, allez à l'escart:
Je ne veulx pas perdre ainsi ma jeunesse
      En languissant.

Marot was widely acclaimed in his day as the greatest of living poets. His output was vast, including *chants royaux, ballades, chansons* (like the Psalms, in varied lyric strophes that were an inspiring novelty) and *rondeaux* (most of these earlier works were collected in the 1532 publication *L'Adolescence Clémentine*); epistles, amorous elegies and epigrams; dozens of formal pieces in observance of royal victories, funerals and so on; translations from Latin and Italian; and much more. Not all of this production is equally memorable, but the best of it is an inalienable possession of the French spirit. "De la jeune Dame" is *rondeau* number 9.

Of the Young Lady Who Has an Old Husband

Languishing and in heavy sadness
Lives my weary heart, once full of joy,
Since I have been given an old man for a husband.
Ah, why? He knows nothing of the ancient art
Taught by Venus, the goddess of love.
    Desiring to show him my abilities,
Often I assail him—but he asks: "What's wrong?"
Or sleeps, perhaps, and my heart lies awake by itself,
    Languishing.
    Then when I want to deceive him,
Shame says to me: "Stop, my girl, stop!
Don't do it, have a care for your honor!"
Then I answer: "Shame, away with you:
I don't want to waste my youth thus
    Languishing."

MAURICE SCÈVE

Born in Lyons, c. 1500; died there, c. 1560

THE first half of the sixteenth century was the most creative
period in the history of Lyons. As wealthy, lively and cultured
as Paris itself, Lyons sheltered a unique group of self-supporting
bourgeois literati, in close personal touch with the latest Italian
trends, who form a link in time between the subsidized courtier-
poets of Marot's school and those of the *Pléiade*.

The unchallenged dean of these Lyons writers was Maurice
Scève, son of a well-to-do judge and councillor, and its undisputed
masterpiece, published in 1544, was Scève's *Delie, Object de plus
haulte vertu* (Delia, Object of Highest Virtue), a cycle of 449
dizains (traditional ten-line strophes) introduced by one *huitain*
(eight-line strophe). Enough Italian Platonism permeates the work
to justify interpreting the loved one's pseudonym partially as an
anagram of *l'Idée*, but basically she is identified with the Greco-
Roman Delia, a fusion of the huntress Diana (whose weapons the
poet readily transforms into Love's arrows), the distant and chaste
moon (who illuminates the night of the poet's learned ignorance)
and funereal Hecate.

These introspective examinations of the fleshly and spiritual
pains of an impossible love reflect Petrarch's influence (in 1533 at
Avignon Scève had discovered a tomb that was supposedly
"Laura's"). Scève's ardor is genuine, however: although reminis-
cences of a former love (the *"lyesse premiere"* of dizain XXIV) are
present in the cycle, his true Delia was undoubtedly the talented
—and married—poetess Pernette du Guillet, who died, at about
twenty-five, the year after *Delie* was published. Scève's style is a
highly personal decoction of the many literary elements he laid
under contribution.

Admired, if not understood, when it first appeared, and recognized by the members of the nascent *Pléiade* as a living example of their own newly expressed ideals (Scève was invited to join the group but declined), *Delie* was branded for centuries as obscure, mystical, cabbalistic or simply "unreadable." It has come into its own, however, within our time; its bold images, its psychological dichotomies and its "dark" beauties strike responsive chords in our twentieth-century sensibilities.

Scève's other important works include the *Saulsaye, églogue de la Vie Solitaire* (The Willow Grove, Eclogue of the Solitary Life; 1547), in praise of the healing charms of nature, and the *Microcosme* (published posthumously in 1562), a poem in 3,003 alexandrines honoring the scientific and artistic achievements of man.

Delie

XXIV

Quand l'œil aux champs est d'esclairs esblouy,
Luy semble nuict quelque part qu'il regarde:
Puis peu à peu de clarté resjouy,
Des soubdains feuz du Ciel se contregarde.
    Mais moy conduict dessoubs la sauvegarde
De ceste tienne, et unique lumière,
Qui m'offusca ma lyesse premiere
Par tes doulx rayz aiguement suyviz,
Ne me pers plus en veue coustumiere.
    Car seulement pour t'adorer je vis.

He also translated (in prose) a Spanish novel based on characters from Boccaccio (1534), and was adjudged the best *blasonneur* of the female body, in Marot's contest, for his "Sourcil" ("a wofull ballad/ Made to his Mistresse eye-brow") after also submitting *blasons* on the forehead, the tear, the throat and the sigh (1536). He composed Latin and French verses on the death of the elder son of François I (1536); wrote the *compte-rendu* of the festive *entrée* of Henri II into Lyons in 1548, which Scève had himself conceived and organized; and produced two Psalm translations and several sonnets, epitaphs and short dedicatory poems, contributing a particularly charming complimentary piece to the first edition of the works of his friend Louise Labé.

Delia

XXIV

When in the fields the eye is dazzled by lightning,
It seems to find night wherever it looks;
Then by degrees, rejoicing in regained sight,
It guards itself against the sudden fires of Heaven.
  But I, led beneath the safeguard
Of that unique light of yours,
Which blinded my early joy
With your ardently pursued sweet rays,
No longer am lost in ordinary sight.
  For I live only to adore you.

Line 8: The rendering "By your sweet rays following in rapid succession" has been proposed.

LOISE LABBÉ LIONNOISE

15 ‡ 55
P W

LOUISE LABÉ

Born in Lyons, c. 1522; died there, 1566

A FÊTED beauty, an accomplished scholar and linguist, a spirited horsewoman, a champion of women's rights and a gifted literary hostess, as well as a touching poet, Louise Labé was one of the chief attractions of Lyons in its brightest days. There is no conclusive evidence that she carried her emulation of famous contemporary Italian poetesses so far as to become herself, though married, a *cortigiana onesta* (courtesan to the élite) in her own city, but her works reveal beyond a doubt that she was consumed by at least one non-conjugal flame (the poet Olivier de Magny ?).

Louise Labé (or Labbé, Charly, Charlin—there are even more variants) was born some time between 1520 and 1524, very possibly in 1522. Her father, Pierre Labé, was a prosperous ropemaker, and so was Ennemond Perrin, the man (much older than herself) she married some time before 1542—hence her famous nickname "la Belle Cordière" (the beautiful ropemaker's wife).

Her literary opus, published in one volume, prefaced by a collection of poems in her honor, in 1555, is not large but it is rich. It consists of a prose *Débat de Folie et d'Amour* (Debate of Folly and Love), which pleads learnedly but gaily for a more than merely cerebral celebration of the ruling passion; three elegies; and twenty-four sonnets (one in Italian). Her poems touch on her dissatisfaction with women's ordinary domestic duties, her adoration of one or more perfect men and her anguish at his/their wanton and cruel absence. The final sonnet, "Ne reprenez, Dames" (Do not blame me, ladies), addressed to the correct and proper women of Lyons, is a heartfelt and unhypocritical answer to the real and exceedingly caustic charges leveled against her.

33

The poetess lost her husband some time after 1559. Lyons, afflicted by economic troubles and religious hatreds, was no longer the luminous place of her youth when Louise, lonelier now, died in 1566.

Sonnet XXIV

Ne reprenez, Dames, si j'ay aymé,
Si j'ay senti mile torches ardentes,
Miles travaus, mile douleurs mordentes.
Si, en pleurant, j'ay mon tems consumé,

Las! que mon nom ne soit par vous blamé.
Si j'ay failli, les peines sont presentes,
N'aigrissez point leurs pointes violentes:
Mais estimez qu'amour, à point nommé,

Sans votre ardeur d'un Vulcan excuser,
Sans la beauté d'Adonis acuser,
Pourra, s'il veut, plus vous rendre amoureuses,

En ayant moins que moy d'ocasion,
Et plus d'estrange et forte passion.
Et gardez vous d'estre plus malheureuses!

Sonnet XXIV

Do not blame me, ladies, if I have loved,
If I have felt a thousand burning torches,
A thousand labors, a thousand biting pains.
If I have worn out my days in weeping,

Alas! let my name not be insulted by you.
If I have erred, my penalties are at hand;
Do not embitter their violent barbs,
But consider that love, coming at the right moment,

Without offering Vulcan as an excuse for your ardor,
Without accusing the beauty of Adonis,
Will be able, if he wishes, to plunge you even more
      deeply in love

With less justification than I have,
And with a stranger and stronger passion.
And take care not to be even more unhappy!

JOACHIM DU BELLAY

Born near Liré, Anjou, c. 1522; died in Paris, 1560

E DMUND SPENSER, who translated some of Du Bellay's Roman sonnets into English (*Ruines of Rome, The Visions of Bellay*), saluted the Frenchman as the "first garland of free Poësie/ That *France* brought forth," and other writers from time to time have placed Du Bellay at the head of French sixteenth-century poets, but the consensus of critics of his day and ours gives him official second place, just below Ronsard.

Du Bellay was born into the less wealthy branch of a noble family. His home was in the Anjou region that he was later to honor in his verse. Orphaned at an early age and reared by an unscholarly elder brother, he did not receive the extensive education in the ancient classics enjoyed by some of his poetic colleagues. By 1546 he had gone to Poitiers to study law and had made the encouraging acquaintance of Jacques Peletier of Le Mans, in whose volume of collected poetry (1547) Du Bellay and Ronsard were each represented by one poem, their first in print.

By 1547 Du Bellay had met Ronsard, a distant relative, and had joined him in Paris, where they studied the classics under the noted humanist Jean Dorat. The small group of fellow student-poets clustered about them came to be known as the *Brigade*; only rarely and metaphorically was the term used by which they are known to literary history—the *Pléiade* (a constellation name which had been applied to seven Alexandrian poets in the third century B.C.). In 1549, the same year in which a bad bout with a chronic illness left Du Bellay partially deaf, he published what was to be the manifesto of this new poetic "school": *La Deffence et Illustration de la Langue Françoise*. In this prose pamphlet, written at white heat in response to another *ars poetica* glorifying the school

37

of Marot, Du Bellay first defends the use of French (instead of Latin) in poetry, then tells how to "illustrate," that is, confer distinction on, the language (chiefly by imitating classical poetic genres and diction).

Between 1549 and 1553 Du Bellay published a great variety of poems, including *Olive* (1549 and 1550), the first Petrarchan sonnet cycle in French; the *Vers lyriques* (1549), the first published French odes; and the "Complainte du désespéré," in which he laments with eloquent sincerity the troubles of his life.

Du Bellay's best work dates from his years in Rome as secretary to his uncle, the cardinal Jean Du Bellay, between 1553 and 1557. Returning to Paris without most of the benefits he had hoped for, he published in 1558 four volumes of verse: the *Antiquitez de Rome*, philosophical sonnets on the inconstancy of the world, inspired by the ruins of the Eternal City (the first time the sonnet had been used for non-amorous purposes); the brilliant series of 191 sonnets, *Les Regrets*, partly an expression of homesickness and frustration, partly a pungent satire on Roman *mores* (generally considered Du Bellay's masterpiece); the *Poemata*, Latin poems chronicling a Roman love affair; and the most varied and entertaining of all Du Bellay's collections, the *Divers Jeux Rustiques*. This last collection includes witty portraits of pet animals, a satire on the Petrarchists, a long powerful poem on the life of a Roman courtesan, and a group of "vows" made by rural folk asking favors of deities. Du Bellay freely adapted and expanded these "Vœuz rustiques" (the genre is classical and was often used by the *Pléiade*) from short Latin poems, first published in 1530, by the Venetian diplomat Andrea Navagero (died 1529). "A Venus," the eleventh of the "Vœuz" (and twelfth poem in the entire book of *Jeux*), presented here, is a prime example of the delicacy for which Du Bellay was noted.

Despite his bad health and increasing personal worries, Du Bellay continued writing, and some of the works of his last years—satirical, political and philosophical—are among his finest. He died at his desk of an apoplectic stroke the first day of January, 1560.

A Venus

Ayant apres long desir
Pris de ma doulce ennemie
Quelques arres du plaisir,
Que sa rigueur me denie,
    Je t'offre ces beaux œillets,
Venus, je t'offre ces roses,
Dont les boutons vermeillets
Imitent les levres closes,
    Que j'ay baisé par trois fois,
Marchant tout beau dessoubs l'ombre
De ce buisson, que tu vois:
Et n'ay sceu passer ce nombre,
    Pource que la mere estoit
Aupres de là, ce me semble,
Laquelle nous aguettoit:
De peur encores j'en tremble.
    Or' je te donne des fleurs:
Mais si tu fais ma rebelle
Autant piteuse à mes pleurs,
Comme à mes yeux elle est belle,
    Un Myrte je dediray
Dessus les rives de Loyre,
Et sur l'écorse escriray
Ces quatre vers à ta gloire:
    THENOT SUR CE BORD ICY,
A VENUS SACRE ET ORDONNE
CE MYRTE, ET LUY DONNE AUSSI
CES TROPPEAUX, ET SA PERSONNE.

To Venus

Having, after long desire,
Taken from my sweet enemy
Some tokens of the pleasure
That her severity denies me,
    I offer you these lovely pinks,
Venus, I offer you these roses,
Whose little crimson buds
Mimic the closed lips
    Which I kissed three times,
Walking quietly beneath the shade
Of this bush that you see;
And I could not go beyond that number
    Because her mother was
Nearby, I believe,
And was spying on us:
I still tremble with the fear of it.
    Now I give you flowers:
But if you make my obstinate girl
As merciful to my tears
As she is beautiful to my eyes,
    I shall dedicate a myrtle to you
By the side of the Loire,
And on the bark I shall write
These four verses to your glory:
    THENOT HERE ON THESE BANKS
HALLOWS AND ASSIGNS TO VENUS
THIS MYRTLE, AND GIVES HER ALSO
THESE FLOCKS, AND HIMSELF.

PIERRE DE RONSARD

Born near Vendôme, c. 1524; died at Saint-Cosme, Touraine, 1585

RONSARD is chiefly famous today as one of the great creators of love lyrics. His virtuoso sonnets to Cassandre in the *Amours* (1552), the graceful sonnets to Marie in the *Continuation des Amours* ("Je vous envoye un bouquet," below, is from this 1555 collection) and in the *Nouvelle Continuation des Amours* (1556), the vigorous *Sonets pour Hélène* (1578) written in his later years and the many poems addressed to Astrée, Genèvre and other ladies restate in ever fresh variations the theme of the brevity of youth and love and offer as a reward for beauty the immortality which only the poet can confer. The symbol of the beautiful but short-lived rose recurs constantly in his verses. Where the identity of the ladies he addresses is established, literary historians disagree on the nature of Ronsard's actual relationship with them; the true dedicatee and the real purpose of even some of the most admired pieces are still matters of dispute; while it is historically attested that Ronsard, a court poet to four French kings, wrote many of these love poems on commission for others. And yet these works are convincing and vital, for in them reality and fantasy are fused by Ronsard's Olympian art. Their spontaneity belies the poet's pains, his lifelong revisions of rhythm and wording; their musicality inspired settings by such important contemporary composers as Lassus, Janequin and Le Jeune; and their subtle blend of classical learning and loving observation of nature made Ronsard supreme in his generation and an inspiration to poets throughout Europe.

But Ronsard's love lyrics do not exhaust his riches. His fifty thousand lines of verse contain so much that even today it is impossible to measure completely his contribution to French literature and Western culture. There are his odes (published 1550 and 1552), inspired by Pindar, Horace, and the Anacreontic poets ("Fay refraischir mon vin," included here, is the tenth ode of the second book, 1550). There are his "hymns" (1555 and 1556), verse disquisitions on philosophic and religious problems, a particularly fascinating one being concerned with demonology. There are the eclogues, elegies and masques (the latter very influential in Elizabethan England); noble discourses on the duties of kings and fiery satires against the Huguenots (1561–63); and dozens of pieces in numerous other genres, some new to French literature, some brought to new perfection. Ronsard's only major failure was the unfinished epic *La Franciade* (1572), which exploited the myth of the Trojan origin of the royal line of France. Six editions of the poet's collected works appeared within his lifetime, from 1560 to 1584.

Ronsard was born between 1522 and 1525 (1524 is most likely) in the château of his father Loys, a faithful, trusted courtier. In

"Je vous envoye un bouquet, que ma main"

Je vous envoye un bouquet, que ma main
Vient de trier de ces fleurs épanies;
Qui ne les eust à ce vespre cueillies,
Cheutes à terre elles fussent demain.

Cela vous soit un exemple certain,
Que vos beautez, bien qu'elles soient fleuries,
En peu de tems cherront toutes fletries,
Et, comme fleurs, periront tout soudain.

Le tems s'en va, le tems s'en va, ma Dame,
Las! le tems non, mais nous nous en allons,
Et tost serons estendus sous la lame,

Et des amours, desquelles nous parlons,
Quand serons morts, n'en sera plus nouvelle:
Pource aimez moy, cependant qu'estes belle.

1538 the boy, while serving as a royal page, accompanied the French bride of James V to Scotland. In 1540, after a journey to Alsace as part of a legation, he was left partially deaf by a severe illness—like Du Bellay, whom he met a few years later and who studied with him under Dorat. Though he was never ordained, Ronsard had received the tonsure, thus becoming eligible for a variety of ecclesiastical benefices dispensed by the kings he served; in addition, he became royal chaplain in 1559. As the acknowledged leader of the *Pléiade*, Ronsard saw his star rise constantly under Henri II, François II (whose widow, Mary Stuart, was a loyal friend of the poet) and Charles IX. In his later years, however, under Henri III, Ronsard's popularity waned—his chief rival being the young Philippe Desportes—and he spent much of his time in rural retirement. The poems published posthumously in 1586 and 1587 prove that the master had retained his creative power to the end.

"I send you a bouquet which with my own hands"

I send you a bouquet which with my own hands
I've just now gathered from these full-blown flowers;
If they had not been picked this evening,
They would have fallen to the ground tomorrow.

Let this be a sure lesson to you,
That your charms, though they are in their bloom,
In a short while will fall completely withered
And, like flowers, will perish quite suddenly.

Time passes on, time passes on, my Lady—
Alas! not time, but we pass on,
And soon we shall be laid beneath the tombstone,

And of the love of which we are speaking,
When we are dead there will be no more tidings:
Therefore love me while you are beautiful.

45

"*Fay refraischir mon vin de sorte*"

Fay refraischir mon vin de sorte
Qu'il passe en froideur un glaçon;
Fay venir Janne, qu'elle apporte
Son luth pour dire une chanson:
Nous ballerons tous trois au son;
Et dy à Barbe qu'elle vienne,
Les cheveux tors à la façon
D'une follastre Italienne.
Ne vois-tu que le jour se passe?
Je ne vy point au lendemain.
Page, reverse dans ma tasse,
Que ce grand verre soit tout plain.
Maudit soit qui languit en vain,
Ces vieux Medecins je n'appreuve:
Mon cerveau n'est jamais bien sain,
Si beaucoup de vin ne l'abreuve.

"Have my wine chilled so that"

Have my wine chilled so that
It surpasses an icicle in coldness;
Have Joan come, let her bring
Her lute to perform a song:
We shall all three dance to her playing.
And tell Barbara to come,
Her hair twisted in the style
The madcap Italian girls wear.
    Can't you see that the day is passing?
I don't live for tomorrow.
Page, replenish the wine in my cup,
Let this tall glass be full to the brim.
Curse the man who languishes in vain;
I don't agree with these old Physicians:
My brain is never fully sound
Unless it is flooded with much wine.

FRANÇOIS DE MALHERBE GENTILHOMME ORDINAIRE DE LA CHAMBRE DV ROY.

FRANÇOIS DE MALHERBE

Born in or near Caen, 1555; died in Paris, 1628

COMING two literary generations after Ronsard and indebted in many ways to this great predecessor's example (not least in his similar conception of the poet's lofty mission in society), Malherbe devoted a lifetime of awesome energy to combating the diction and prosody of Ronsard's *Pléiade* and to establishing himself as the arbiter of taste in spoken and written French. Malherbe never composed a formal treatise on poetry. Many of his principles can be gleaned from his unfavorable commentary (which he never published) on the works of Desportes, Ronsard's successor as court poet, and from numerous anecdotes that illustrate Malherbe's intransigent character and bludgeon-like wit. The chief text of Malherbe's great "reform," however, is his own poetic opus, a living monument to the purification of vocabulary and regularization of lines and stanzas he sought.

Despite determined opposition from various quarters, Malherbe's principles of euphony were to dominate French poetry for two hundred years. But though his followers found it easy to imitate his negative prescriptions, few matched the natural elegance of his style, his fine sense of word placement and the vigorous rhythms that pulse through his best stanzas.

The path toward perfection and recognition was slow. Born in or near Caen, Malherbe, son of a magistrate, studied at Paris, Heidelberg and Basel, as well as in his native Normandy. Desirous of military glory and a place at the royal court, in 1576 he joined the retinue of Henri Valois, a natural son of Henri II, who was sent almost immediately afterward to quell Huguenot uprisings in Provence. There Malherbe became the oracle of literary circles. After the murder of his master in 1586 he lived at Caen once more until 1595, then chiefly in Provence for ten more years. In 1600, when he wrote his great ode on the arrival in France of Marie de Médicis, bride of Henri IV, he was mentioned to the king as the greatest poet in France, but he did not finally leave Provence and become accepted at court until 1605, at the age of fifty.

In his new position, his ascendancy was phenomenal, and the bulk of his output dates from his years as court poet. This includes lengthy official odes (to Henri IV, later to Marie as regent and to the young Louis XIII); amorous and flattering sonnets; texts for pageants; long, rather rigid love poems in a variety of stanza forms (*stances*); "consolations" to friends on mournful occasions; and Psalm paraphrases, like the late one (first published 1626) included here.

Malherbe's only surviving child, the son born in 1600, was killed in an irregular duel in 1627. After that Malherbe spent the little that remained of his own life trying in vain to persuade Louis XIII to take extreme measures against the assailants. He even followed the king to the siege of La Rochelle in the summer of 1628. This strain was too much for the spirited old man, who died in October of that year.

Imitation du Pseaume

LAUDA ANIMA MEA DOMINUM

N'esperons plus, mon ame, aux promesses du monde:
Sa lumiere est un verre, et sa faveur une onde,
Que tousjours quelque vent empesche de calmer;
Quittons ces vanitez, lassons-nous de les suivre:
    C'est Dieu qui nous faict vivre,
    C'est Dieu qu'il faut aimer.

En vain, pour satisfaire à nos lasches envies,
Nous passons pres des rois tout le temps de nos vies,
A souffrir des mespris et ployer les genoux;
Ce qu'ils peuvent n'est rien: ils sont comme nous sommes,
    Veritablement hommes,
    Et meurent comme nous.

Ont-ils rendu l'esprit, ce n'est plus que poussiere
Que cette majesté si pompeuse et si fiere
Dont l'esclat orgueilleux estonne l'univers;
Et dans ces grands tombeaux où leurs ames hautaines
    Font encore les vaines,
    Ils sont mangez des vers.

Là se perdent ces noms de maistres de la terre,
D'arbitres de la paix, de foudres de la guerre:
Comme ils n'ont plus de sceptre, ils n'ont plus de flatteurs,
Et tombent avecque eux d'une cheute commune
    Tous ceux que leur fortune
    Faisoit leurs serviteurs.

Paraphrase of the Psalm

LAUDA ANIMA MEA DOMINUM

Let us trust no longer, my soul, in the world's promises;
Its light is a glass, and its favor a wave
Which some wind always prevents us from calming.
Let us abandon these vanities, let us tire of following them;
    It is God who gives us life,
    It is God we must love.

In vain, to satisfy our craven desires,
We spend all the days of our life in the presence of kings,
Suffering scorn and bending our knee;
What they are capable of, is as nothing: they are, as we are,
    Truly mortals,
    And die like us.

When they have given up the ghost, only dust remains
Of that majesty so stately and so haughty,
Whose prideful brilliance made the universe marvel:
And in those vast tombs where their arrogant souls
    Are still piqued with vanity,
    They are eaten by worms.

There they lose those titles of masters of the earth,
Arbiters of peace, thunderbolts of war;
Since they have no more scepter, they have no more flatterers;
And toppled with them in a general fall
    Are all those whom their fortune
    Once made their servants.

This is Psalm 145 in the Vulgate, 146 in the King James version.

53

LES
OEVVRES,
ET
SVITTE DES
OEVVRES
DV SIEVR
DE
SAINT-AMANT.

SECONDE EDITION,
Reueüe, corrigée & augmentée de nouueau.

❧

A PARIS,
Chez NICOLAS TRABOVLLIET, au
Palais, en la Gallerie des Prisonniers,
à la Tulippe.

M. DC. XXXIII.
AVEC PRIVILEGE DV ROY.

MARC-ANTOINE GÉRARD DE SAINT-AMANT

Born in Rouen, 1594; died in Paris, 1661

SAINT-AMANT, son of a Rouen merchant, was the most colorful and unusual figure among seventeenth-century French poets. In an era of cabals and coteries, he maintained friendships in almost every literary, political and religious camp, though he was not independently wealthy. His travels (many in the entourage of some noble patron) took him to many countries: to West Africa and the Caribbean (before 1620); twice to England (1631, 1643, his long poem *Albion* and several short pieces decrying the shameless nation that attacked its own king); to Italy (1633, the trip resulting in the *Rome ridicule*, a burlesque disparagement of the famous Roman monuments and legends); to the Mediterranean on a naval expedition (1636–37, recounted in *Le Passage de Gibraltar*); and, at the age of fifty-five, across northern Europe to the courts of Poland and Sweden (1649–51). His interest in science and philosophy led him to visit Campanella and Galileo while in Italy, as well as the tomb of Copernicus while on his way to Warsaw.

Saint-Amant's range of forms and genres is exceptional: from the epigram and sonnet through *rondeaux*, triolets, elegies, epistles, satires, odes and works in a variety of stanzas to the biblical epic *Moyse sauvé* (Moses Saved, 1653). The baroque diversity of his themes and subjects embraces the frequenting of haunted ruins (especially in "La Solitude"); the first seascapes in French literature; the pleasures of the pipe, the table, the bed; the current events of many stirring years; and religious meditations. His extravagant vocabulary includes naval and scientific terms, witty nonce words and scurrilous monosyllables. His chief goals were originality, imagination, inspiration.

The tone Saint-Amant strikes most often is that of sportive irreverence. He delights especially in painting himself as one of a group of poetic *bons vivants*, addicted to tobacco, cheered by wine or cider, literally enraptured by a fine melon, a huge ham or a creamy and evil-smelling cheese. The sonnet "Le Paresseux"— a hymn to sloth, concomitant of debauch—was first published in *La Suitte* (Continuation) *des Œuvres* (1631), the second collection of the poet's works. The first collection, *Les Œuvres*, had appeared in 1629; later collections included the *Seconde Partie des Œuvres*,

Le Paresseux

Accablé de paresse et de melancholie,
Je resve dans un lict où je suis fagoté
Comme un lievre sans os qui dort dans un pasté,
Ou comme un Dom-Quichot en sa morne folie.

Là, sans me soucier des guerres d'Italie,
Du comte Palatin, ny de sa royauté,
Je consacre un bel hymne à cette oisiveté
Où mon ame en langueur est comme ensevelie.

Je trouve ce plaisir si doux et si charmant,
Que je croy que les biens me viendront en dormant,
Puis que je voy des-jà s'en enfler ma bedaine,

Et hay tant le travail, que, les yeux entr'ouverts,
Une main hors des draps, cher BAUDOIN, à peine
Ay-je pû me resoudre à t'escrire ces vers.

1643, the *Troisième Partie*, 1649, and the *Dernier Recueil* (Last Collection) in 1658. Several poems were published separately.

Saint-Amant, who was thoroughly familiar with the contemporary literature of Italy and Spain, mentions the adventures of Don Quixote in other poems besides "Le Paresseux." The poet Jean Baudoin to whom the sonnet is addressed was to become, in 1634, along with Saint-Amant himself, a founding member of the Académie Française.

The Lazy Poet

Overwhelmed with sloth and melancholy,
I dream in a bed in which I am trussed up
Like a boned hare sleeping in a pie,
Or like Don Quixote in his gloomy madness.

There, not worrying about the Italian wars,
The Count Palatine or his royalty,
I dedicate a fine hymn to that idleness
In which my languishing soul is practically buried.

I find this pleasure so sweet and charming,
That I think all good things will come to me while I sleep,
Since I already see my belly swelling with them;

And I hate work so much that, with my eyes half-closed,
With one hand out of the sheets, my dear Baudoin, I scarcely
Was able to bring myself to write you these verses.

JEAN DE LA FONTAINE

Born in Château-Thierry, 1621; died in Paris, 1695

THE greatest lyricist of France's Golden Age, La Fontaine has often been considered the greatest French poet of all. Not only are his *Fables* quoted, consciously or otherwise, in every-day French conversation as often as Shakespeare in English daily speech; but La Fontaine is also the poet's poet for his many excellences: for his ingenious and unique manipulation of *vers libres* (lines of varying numbers of syllables not arranged in any fixed stanza pattern), for the polish and ease of his expression, for his variety, his sparkle, his sensitivity of technique and of feeling. He has been blasted as a cynical egoist, cherished as a tender-hearted *naïf*; branded a simpleton, credited with the most acute diplomatic perspicacity: very few have questioned his supreme esthetic merit.

La Fontaine was born in 1621. In 1641 he entered the Congregation of the Oratory in Paris, but left the next year. He also studied law in the capital during his twenties. Back in his native Château-Thierry, he married in 1647, but was apparently never a devoted husband. He succeeded his father, who died leaving heavy debts, in his post as the local administrator of forests (until 1671); opinions vary as to just how poorly he fulfilled his duties. In the late 1650's he received a poet's pension from the finance minister Fouquet, for whom, in happy days, he wrote his "Adonis" and the (never completed) prose and verse *Songe de Vaux*—Dream of Vaux (Fouquet's estate). In the hard days after the minister's fall from grace in 1661, La Fontaine wrote the so-called "Élégie des Nymphes de Vaux" and the "Ode au Roi," both loyally imploring the clemency of Louis XIV.

In 1663 the poet made a trip to Limoges with an exiled uncle, sending six delightful travel letters to his wife. The next years, during which he entered the household of the dowager Duchess of Orleans in Paris, marked the appearance of his first *Contes et nouvelles en vers* (Verse Tales and Novellas, 1665, 1666, 1671, 1674); these, immensely popular, were new versions of licentious anecdotes from Boccaccio, the *Heptameron* and other Italian and French sources.

The *Fables*, also instantly acclaimed, were the fruit of La Fontaine's maturity and old age. The first six books, containing over 120 fables based chiefly on the classical fabulists and (only relatively to the later ones) unadorned and impersonal, appeared in 1668. The next group, comprising what is today Books VII through XI—over 85 fables based on a wider variety of sources and featuring a much fuller personal participation of the poet as moralist, philosopher (interesting polemics against Descartes's mechanistic conception of animal behavior), literary craftsman and amused observer—appeared in 1678 and 1679; the 27 fables of Book XII in 1693. "Le Savetier et le Financier," included here, is the second fable of Book VIII. It would take a volume longer than the present one to analyze adequately the humor, the character studies, the

Le Savetier et le Financier

Un Savetier chantoit du matin jusqu'au soir;
    C'étoit merveilles de le voir,
Merveilles de l'ouïr; il faisoit des passages,
    Plus content qu'aucun des sept sages.
Son voisin, au contraire, étant tout cousu d'or,
    Chantoit peu, dormoit moins encor;
    C'étoit un homme de finance.
Si, sur le point du jour, parfois il sommeilloit,
Le Savetier alors en chantant l'éveilloit;
    Et le Financier se plaignoit
    Que les soins de la Providence
N'eussent pas au marché fait vendre le dormir,
    Comme le manger et le boire.

appreciation of nature, the mellow acceptance of life, the infinite felicities that await the reader of the *Fables*.

After the death of the Duchess in 1672, La Fontaine was the guest of Madame de La Sablière for some twenty years. After she too died, in 1693, the poet, whose health was beginning to fail, enjoyed the hospitality of the d'Hervart home, where he died in 1695. In 1683 he had been elected to the Académie Française; the king opposed his admission until the next year, when a new vacancy made it possible for Boileau, who had Louis's blessing, to be admitted as well. In his last years La Fontaine, who had written several pious works earlier, became more openly religious and even made a public renunciation of his *Contes* in 1693.

La Fontaine's versatile *œuvre* also includes love elegies, superb verse epistles on his own character and poetic credo, operatic librettos (and the documentation of a quarrel with Lulli), plays, epigrams, a poetic disquisition on quinine, a long retelling in prose and verse of Apuleius' Cupid and Psyche story, famous epitaphs for Molière (1673) and for himself, and many short pieces.

The Cobbler and the Financier

A Cobbler used to sing from morning to evening;
　　It was wonderful to see him,
Wonderful to hear him; he would perform cadenzas,
　　Happier than any of the seven sages.
His neighbor, on the other hand, who was rolling in money,
　　Sang very little, slept even less;
　　He was a man of finance.
If, at daybreak, he sometimes dozed a bit,
Then the Cobbler would awaken him by singing;
　　And the Financier complained
　　That the plans of Providence
Had not arranged for sleep to be sold in the marketplace
　　Like food and drink.

En son hôtel il fait venir
Le chanteur, et lui dit: "Or çà, sire Grégoire,
Que gagnez-vous par an? — Par an? Ma foi, Monsieur,
   Dit, avec un ton de rieur,
Le gaillard Savetier, ce n'est point ma manière
De compter de la sorte; et je n'entasse guère
  Un jour sur l'autre: il suffit qu'à la fin
    J'attrape le bout de l'année;
    Chaque jour amène son pain.
— Eh bien, que gagnez-vous, dites-moi, par journée?
— Tantôt plus, tantôt moins: le mal est que toujours
(Et sans cela nos gains seroient assez honnêtes),
Le mal est que dans l'an s'entremêlent des jours
    Qu'il faut chommer; on nous ruine en fêtes;
L'une fait tort à l'autre; et Monsieur le curé
De quelque nouveau saint charge toujours son prône."
Le Financier, riant de sa naïveté,
Lui dit: "Je vous veux mettre aujourd'hui sur le
    trône.
Prenez ces cent écus; gardez-les avec soin,
   Pour vous en servir au besoin."
Les Savetier crut voir tout l'argent que la terre
    Avoit, depuis plus de cent ans,
    Produit pour l'usage des gens.
Il retourne chez lui; dans sa cave il enserre
    L'argent, et sa joie à la fois.
    Plus de chant: il perdit la voix,
Du moment qu'il gagna ce qui cause nos peines.
    Le sommeil quitta son logis;
    Il eut pour hôtes les soucis,
    Les soupçons, les alarmes vaines;
Tout le jour, il avoit l'œil au guet; et la nuit,
    Si quelque chat faisoit du bruit,
Le chat prenoit l'argent. A la fin le pauvre homme
S'en courut chez celui qu'il ne réveilloit plus:
"Rendez-moi, lui dit-il, mes chansons et mon somme,
    Et reprenez vos cent écus."

He summoned the singer
To his mansion, and said to him: "Look here, Master Gregory,
What do you earn per year?" "Per year? My goodness, Sir,"
      Said the merry Cobbler
With laughter in his voice, "I don't generally
Count my earnings that way; and I don't pile up
   One day's receipts on another's; it's enough if finally
      I make ends meet when the year is over;
      Every day brings in some bread."
"Well then, tell me, what do you earn per day?"
"Sometimes more, sometimes less: the trouble is that always
(And otherwise our income would be quite respectable),
The trouble is that during the year days are mixed in
   When we have to sit idle; they ruin us with holidays;
One holiday drives out the other; and the priest
Is always burdening his sermon with some new saint."
The Financier, laughing at his simplicity,
Said to him: "Today I shall place you on the throne.
Take this hundred crowns; guard it with care
      So you can use it when necessary."
The Cobbler thought he saw all the money that the earth
      Had, for over a hundred years,
      Produced for the use of man.
He returned home; in his cellar he locked up
      The money, and his joy at the same time.
      No more singing: he lost his voice
The moment he acquired the cause of our woes.
      Sleep abandoned his dwelling;
      He had for guests worries,
      Suspicions, false alarms;
All day he kept a sharp lookout; and at night
      If some cat made noise,
The cat was taking the money. Finally the poor man
Ran to the home of the one he no longer awakened:
"Give me back," he said, "my songs and my sleep,
      And take back your hundred crowns."

FRANÇOIS-MARIE AROUET, DIT VOLTAIRE

Born in Paris, 1694; died there, 1778

IT is Voltaire's prose that is generally read today—his amusing philosophic tales, his *Dictionnaire philosophique*, his voluminous correspondence and the historical works in which he was among the first to practice historiography and philosophy of history as these disciplines are understood today. But for the greater part of his life he considered himself primarily as a poet. And even if we do not include the many verse tragedies of which he was so proud, still in his numerous poetic epigrams, satires, odes, epistles, "tales," philosophic poems, epics and occasional pieces Voltaire emerges as the most representative, as well as the most important, poet of the Regency and the reign of Louis XV, an era, unfortunately, in which serious poems seemed very close to rhymed prose and less solemn poems rarely rose above the level of very light verse.

Poetic landmarks are found throughout the course of Voltaire's agitated existence. They register the amorous adventures of the brilliant young bourgeois, son of a Parisian notary, in the company of his titled classmates; the early political lampooning and two sojourns in the Bastille (1717 and 1726); the various exiles from Paris, including the long stay in England (1726–29) during which Voltaire completed the *Henriade*, an epic on the life and times of Henri IV; the scientific studies of the years at Cirey (Champagne) with Madame du Châtelet; the period of royal recognition in Paris (election to the Académie Française, 1746); the glory and the disappointments of the court of Frederick the Great (1750–53); the all but final detachment from Paris as *persona non grata*; the Geneva interlude and active old age (1758–78) at Ferney (not far from Switzerland); and the triumphal return to Paris in 1778.

The variety of this poetic production will be evident from the briefest selection of titles: "Le Pour et le Contre" (Pro and Con, 1722), a reflection on religion, with a preference for deism; "Le Temple du Goût" (The Temple of Taste, 1732, alternating verse and prose), an inquiry into literary taste and an evaluation of the seventeenth-century poets; "Le Mondain" (The Worldling, 1736), an epicurean appreciation of the present moment; the "Poème sur la loi naturelle" (Poem on Natural Law, 1752); *La Pucelle* (The Maid, 1755), a long mock-epic about Joan of Arc; and the "Poème sur le désastre de Lisbonne" (1756), on the earthquake of 1755.

But the genres in which Voltaire, like his contemporaries, was most successful were those in which he captured the verve and

Les " Vous" et les " Tu"

Philis, qu'est devenu ce temps
Où, dans un fiacre promenée,
Sans laquais, sans ajustements,
De tes grâces seules ornée,
Contente d'un mauvais soupé
Que tu changeais en ambroisie,
Tu te livrais, dans ta folie,
A l'amant heureux et trompé
Qui t'avait consacré sa vie?

Le ciel ne te donnait alors,
Pour tout rang et pour tous trésors,
Que les agréments de ton âge,
Un cœur tendre, un esprit volage,
Un sein d'albâtre, et de beaux yeux.
Avec tant d'attraits précieux,
Hélas! qui n'eût été friponne?
Tu le fus, objet gracieux;
Et (que l'Amour me le pardonne!)
Tu sais que je t'en aimais mieux.

sparkle of the Rococo age. Among these lighter poems, his epistles are perhaps the finest, and none more so than the "Épître connue sous le nom des 'Vous' et des 'Tu'" (Epistle 33, composed about 1730), in which the poet makes brilliant use of the familiar and the formal "you" for humorous and psychological ends. The "Philis" addressed had been an actress and a mistress of the poet, who had presented her with the portrait of himself (reproduced here) painted in 1718 by Nicolas de Largillière. When "Philis" married a marquis, her door was closed to Voltaire; hence this poem. They were to meet again, both in their eighties and the Marquise now a widow, when Voltaire finally reached Paris again shortly before his death. "Philis" still owned the portrait.

"Vous" and "Tu"

Phyllis, what has become of the days
When, out riding in a carriage,
Without lackeys, without trappings,
Adorned only by your graces,
Content with a poor supper,
Which you changed into ambrosia,
You abandoned yourself, in your gaiety,
To the happy deceived lover
Who had devoted his life to you?

Heaven gave you then
As the sum total of rank and treasures
Only the charms of your youth,
A tender heart, a flighty mind,
An alabaster breast, and beautiful eyes.
With so many precious allurements,
Ah! what girl would not have been mischievous?
You were so, graceful creature,
And (Love pardon me for this!)
You know I loved you all the more for it.

Ah, madame! que votre vie,
D'honneurs aujourd'hui si remplie,
Diffère de ces doux instants!
Ce large suisse à cheveux blancs,
Qui ment sans cesse à votre porte,
Philis, est l'image du Temps:
On dirait qu'il chasse l'escorte
Des tendres Amours et des Ris:
Sous vos magnifiques lambris
Ces enfants tremblent de paraître.
Hélas! je les ai vus jadis
Entrer chez toi par la fenêtre
Et se jouer dans ton taudis.

Non, madame, tous ces tapis
Qu'a tissus la Savonnerie,
Ceux que les Persans ont ourdis,
Et toute votre orfèvrerie,
Et ces plats si chers que Germain
A gravés de sa main divine,
Et ces cabinets où Martin
A surpassé l'art de la Chine;
Vos vases japonais et blancs,
Toutes ces fragiles merveilles;
Ces deux lustres de diamants
Qui pendent à vos deux oreilles;
Ces riches carcans, ces colliers,
Et cette pompe enchanteresse,
Ne valent pas un des baisers
Que tu donnais dans ta jeunesse.

Ah, Madame! how your life,
Today so filled with honors,
Differs from those sweet moments!
This hulking doorkeeper with powdered hair
Who tells incessant lies at your door,
Phyllis, is the image of Time:
One could say he drives away the escort
Of tender Loves and Laughter;
Those children tremble to show their face
Beneath your magnificent paneled ceilings.
Alas! in former days I saw them
Enter your home through the window
And frolic in your hovel.

No, Madame, all those carpets
Woven at the Savonnerie,
Those which the Persians loomed,
And all your gold jewelry,
And those expensive plates which Germain
Engraved with his divine hand,
And those cabinets in which Martin
Has outdone the art of China;
Your Japanese and white vases,
All those fragile wonders;
Those two diamond pendants
Hanging from your two ears;
Those costly chokers, those necklaces,
And that spellbinding pomp,
Are not worth one of the kisses
You gave when you were young.

ANDRÉ CHÉNIER

Born in Constantinople, 1762; died in Paris, 1794

THE dewy freshness of his language, the plasticity of his scenes and images, the boldness of his versification and the vigor pulsing through each emotion he communicates set André Chénier apart from the other poets of his time, whose ideals and mannerisms he nevertheless shares to a great extent. Born in Constantinople (his father was a French businessman and diplomat who had married a Levantine woman), Chénier never saw the Greek world again after his infancy, though he often longed to return. But Greece remained for him a beacon, the home of truth. His profound and sensitive studies of the ancient authors inspired Chénier's luminous poetic re-creations of the Greek countryside, and even molded his attitudes toward art and life.

The poet's father brought the family to France in 1765. André lived with relatives in and near Carcassonne for about eight years. From 1773 to about 1781 he attended the exclusive Collège de Navarre in Paris, where he became the friend and companion of several young nobles, "enlightened" in politics and libertine in morals. For six months in 1782–83 Chénier was with a regiment at Strasbourg, hoping in vain for a commission. After his return to Paris, he became seriously ill (his ardent sexual adventures were often interrupted by painful kidney and bladder ailments), and in 1784 he made a journey to Switzerland for his health. Another trip in the company of his wealthy friends, in 1786, was to have ended in Constantinople, but the travelers got no farther than Italy. From 1787 to 1790 Chénier was in England, unhappy, as the personal secretary of the French ambassador. Returning home after the outbreak of the Revolution, he joined, as orator and journalist, the moderate political group who became known as the "Feuillants." Like his friends in the nobility, Chénier was not averse to the abolition of feudal taxes and privileges, but he was a Royalist, an enemy of indiscipline and disorder and a vociferous opponent of the Jacobins. After August 1792 Chénier stayed out of the public eye, journeying to Rouen and Le Havre, spending most of 1793 at Versailles. But his past friction with the Jacobins and his continued frequenting of suspicious people led ultimately to his arrest on March 7, 1794, and his execution on July 28 of that year, the day after Robespierre's fall announced the end of the Terror.

Only two of Chénier's poems were published in his lifetime, both inspired by current events of the Revolution and neither among his best work. The rest of his poetry was known only to a few friends. (No sizable portion of his manuscripts was published until 1819.) Most of the pieces were left, at Chénier's death, unfinished or without final polishing. There are only fragments of his vast projects for encyclopedic didactic poems, but even as they stand, these, and the numerous elegies (the most famous of which is "La jeune Tarentine"), idyls, epistles, hymns, odes (one in celebration of Charlotte Corday), epigrams and other works comprise an inexhaustible treasure.

Surely the most affecting poems are those Chénier composed in the prison of Saint-Lazare, writing them on small strips of paper and sending them out hidden in his laundry baskets. Among these final works are several in alternating lines of twelve and eight syllables, a scheme referred to as *iambes* and generally used for satirical poetry, in imitation of the satirical iambics of the Greek poet Archilochus. To appreciate more fully the vehemence and bitterness of "Quand au mouton bêlant," which follows, it is necessary to recall not only the vapid pastoral amusements of the eighteenth-century court, but also the earlier works of Chénier himself, in which the life of sheep and of shepherds had denoted only peace and love.

"*Quand au mouton bêlant la sombre boucherie*"

Quand au mouton bêlant la sombre boucherie
    Ouvre ses cavernes de mort,
Pâtres, chiens et moutons, toute la bergerie
    Ne s'informe plus de son sort.
Les enfants qui suivaient ses ébats dans la plaine,
    Les vierges aux belles couleurs
Qui le baisaient en foule, et sur sa blanche laine
    Entrelaçaient rubans et fleurs,
Sans plus penser à lui, le mangent s'il est tendre.
    Dans cet abîme enseveli,
J'ai le même destin. Je m'y devais attendre.
    Accoutumons-nous à l'oubli.
Oubliés comme moi dans cet affreux repaire,
    Mille autres moutons, comme moi
Pendus aux crocs sanglants du charnier populaire,
    Seront servis au peuple-roi.
Que pouvaient mes amis? Oui, de leur main chérie
    Un mot, à travers les barreaux,
Eût versé quelque baume en mon âme flétrie,
    De l'or peut-être à mes bourreaux...
Mais tout est précipice. Ils ont eu droit de vivre.
    Vivez, amis, vivez contents.
En dépit de [Fouquier], soyez lents à me suivre;
    Peut-être en de plus heureux temps
J'ai moi-même, à l'aspect des pleurs de l'infortune,
    Détourné mes regards distraits;
A mon tour aujourd'hui mon malheur importune.
    Vivez, amis; vivez en paix.

Line 23: After "de" a two-syllable name is missing in the manuscript; editors often supply the name of Fouquier [-Tinville], the notorious public prosecutor of the Terror.

"When the somber slaughterhouse opens its caverns of death"

When the somber slaughterhouse opens its caverns of death
  To a bleating sheep,
Shepherds, dogs, the other sheep, the whole farm
  Is no longer concerned with its fate.
The children who followed its sporting in the plain,
  The maidens with lovely complexions
Who crowded about to kiss it, and on its white wool
  Tied knots of ribbons and flowers,
Without thinking of it further, eat it if it is tender.
  Buried in this abyss,
I have the same destiny. I should have expected it.
  Let us become accustomed to neglect.
Forgotten like me in this frightful lair,
  A thousand other sheep, like me
Hanging from the bloody hooks of the people's larder,
  Will be served up to the Sovereign People.
What could my friends do? Yes, a line written by their beloved
    hands,
  Passed through the bars,
Might have poured some balm on my withered soul;
  Perhaps some gold to my executioners . . .
But all is a precipice. They were right to live.
  Live, friends, live in contentment.
In spite of [Fouquier], be slow to follow me;
  Perchance in happier days
I myself, when seeing tears of misfortune,
  Turned away my eyes distractedly;
Today in its turn my distress is burdensome.
  Live, friends; live in peace.

ALPHONSE DE LAMARTINE

Born in Mâcon, 1790; died at Passy (Paris), 1869

LAMARTINE'S *Méditations poétiques* (1820) has been from its first appearance the most beloved, the archetypal, book of Romantic verse. The poet's diction and versification (as well as his deism) were patterned after eighteenth-century models (and continued to be so throughout his poetic career), but the vague melancholy and the ardent, heartfelt reminiscences of past love expressed in poems like "Le Lac" (The Lake) were the revelation of a new esthetic. Lamartine's readers wanted all his books to be repetitions of the *Méditations* and were openly disappointed as his manner and themes evolved toward more mature statements.

The poet was born at Mâcon in Burgundy. His youth was spent in amorous indolence, since his family, provincial nobles without a great fortune, did not want him to serve Napoleon. When the Restoration came, he undertook a diplomatic career. The year 1820 saw the publication of the *Méditations* (inspired largely by his affair with "Elvire" at Aix-les-Bains in 1816), a fervent return to the Catholic principles of his childhood, his marriage to an Englishwoman and his departure for a post in Naples. Lamartine returned to France the next year.

The *Nouvelles Méditations poétiques* of 1823, which contains the famous "Les Préludes," includes some politically inspired pieces as well as more poems on love and religion. *La Mort de Socrate*, a long poem which depicts Socrates as a prophet of Christianity, appeared in the same year. The *Dernier Chant du Pèlerinage d'Harold* (Last Canto of Childe Harold's Pilgrimage, 1825) was a homage to Byron's memory. From 1825 to 1828 Lamartine served in a diplomatic post in Florence. He was elected to the Académie Française in 1829. The following year he published the *Harmonies poétiques et religieuses*, possibly his richest volume. After the accession of Louis-Philippe in the same year, Lamartine voluntarily ended his diplomatic career, turning to politics instead. His journey to the Near East in 1832–33 (recounted in his prose *Souvenirs d'un voyage en Orient*, 1835) was marred by the death at Beirut of his only surviving child, an event which permanently shook his religious faith.

The last volumes of poetry Lamartine published were *Jocelyn* (1836), a modern "epic" of a priest's life in the Savoy Alps; *La Chute d'un Ange* (The Fall of an Angel, 1838), a lengthy allegorical narrative with a strong biblical tinge, about the upward struggle of the human spirit; and the *Recueillements poétiques* (Poetic Self-Communions, 1839), a mixed collection that contains the poem "La Cloche du village" (The Village Church-Bell), the final stanzas of which are presented here. This poem, a good example of Lamartine's firmer later style, exhibits the rhetorical force, warm sonorities and copious flow of his verse. In the course of the poem, the sound of the village bell on the poet's beloved country estate evokes for him his happy rural boyhood (one of Lamartine's most rewarding themes, recurring in many poems), former days of fame and glory, and finally an obsession with death.

Lamartine had always spoken of himself as an amateur in poetry (he wrote quickly and rarely polished his work, much of which suffers somewhat in this respect) and by 1839 felt that a reputation as a poet might injure his growing reputation as a statesman (he had been a Deputy since 1833). For a few months during the Revolution of 1848 Lamartine, displaying great personal bravery and endurance, was the most influential member of the provisional government, but his socialistic and anticlerical tendencies soon spelled political doom. Out of favor in both the political and literary circles of the Second Empire and burdened with enormous debts, he supported himself during the last twenty years of his life with a steady stream of prose works: history, literary criticism and semi-autobiographical fiction. Some of the poems of his old age (posthumously published) are among his best, particularly "La Vigne et la maison" (The Vine and the House).

La Cloche du village (extrait)

Ne t'étonne donc pas, enfant, si ma pensée,
Au branle de l'airain secrètement bercée,
Aime sa voix mystique et fidèle au trépas,
Si, dès le premier son qūi gémit sous sa voûte,
Sur un pied suspendu je m'arrête, et j'écoute
    Ce que la mort me dit tout bas.

Et toi, saint porte-voix des tristesses humaines,
Que la terre inventa pour mieux crier ses peines,
Chante! des cœurs brisés le timbre est encor beau!
Que ton gémissement donne une âme à la pierre,
Des larmes aux yeux secs, un signe à la prière,
    Une mélodie au tombeau!

*

Moi, quand des laboureurs porteront dans ma bière
Le peu qui doit rester ici de ma poussière;
Après tant de soupirs que mon sein lance ailleurs,
Quand des pleureurs gagés, froide et banale escorte,
Déposeront mon corps endormi sous la porte
    Qui mène à des soleils meilleurs,

Si quelque main pieuse en mon honneur te sonne,
Des sanglots de l'airain, oh! n'attriste personne.
Ne va pas mendier des pleurs à l'horizon;
Mais prends ta voix de fête, et sonne sur ma tombe
Avec le bruit joyeux d'une chaîne qui tombe
    Au seuil libre d'une prison!

Ou chante un air semblable au cri de l'alouette
Qui, s'élevant du chaume où la bise la fouette,
Dresse à l'aube du jour son vol mélodieux,
Et gazouille ce chant qui fait taire d'envie
Ses rivaux attachés aux ronces de la vie,
    Et qui se perd au fond des cieux!

The Village Bell (excerpt)

Do not wonder then, child, if my mind,
Secretly rocked by the swinging of the bronze bell,
Loves its mystic voice that is faithful to death;
If, from the first sound which moans beneath its vault,
I stop with one foot raised and I listen
    To what death tells me in a low voice.

And you, sacred spokesman of human sadness,
Which the earth invented to call out its sorrows more effectively,
Sing! The timbre of broken hearts is still beautiful.
Let your moaning give a soul to the stone,
Tears to dry eyes, a sign to prayer,
    A melody to the tomb!

*

As for me, when plowmen carry within my bier
The little of my dust that is to remain here below;
After so many sighs that my breast hurls elsewhere,
When hired mourners, a cold and banal escort,
Deposit my sleeping body beneath the gate
    That leads to better suns,

If some pious hand rings you in my honor,
Oh! sadden no one with your brazen sobs.
Do not go begging tears from the horizon;
But put on your festival voice, and ring over my tomb
With the joyous noise of a chain falling
    On the free threshold of a prison!

Or sing an air like the call of the lark
Which, rising from the stubble where the wintry wind whips it,
Lifts its melodious flight at the dawn of the day,
And warbles that song which silences with envy
Its rivals attached to the brambles of life,
    And which is lost in the furthest reaches of heaven!

ALFRED DE VIGNY

Born at Loches, Touraine, 1797; died in Paris, 1863

LIKE Lamartine, Vigny was an impoverished petty nobleman of Royalist sympathies (both young poets were in the military escort of the retreating Louis XVIII during the Hundred Days in 1815); but unlike Lamartine, he considered poetry to be the most important thing in life. He wrote slowly and carefully and published relatively little. For Vigny, the poet was the prime example of the genius ill-used by fate and by society; if the genius is not to be destroyed young (like Nicolas Gilbert, Thomas Chatterton and André Chénier in Vigny's 1832 three-part prose work *Stello*), he must develop a stoical attitude and, if need be, cultivate silence (like the exemplary wolf in the poem "La Mort du loup").

Vigny was born in Touraine in 1797, but his family moved to Paris the next year. From 1814 to 1824 he was an army officer serving at various garrisons, constantly disappointed by the lack of opportunities for glory. In his 1835 prose work *Servitude et grandeur militaires* (Bondage and Greatness in the Military Life), often considered his finest book, he praises the military man's capacity for self-sacrifice. Vigny's first poems were published in 1822, "Éloa" in 1824. *Poèmes antiques et modernes* (1826, expanded editions 1829, 1837) contains all the poems Vigny finally collected for publication during his lifetime. Well-known poems in this volume are "Moïse" (Moses, written 1823), about the burdens and solitude of a great leader, and "Le Cor" (The Horn, written 1826), a picturesque scene in the Pyrenees with an evocation of the death of Roland. With the poems in this collection Vigny justly claimed to have introduced the genre of the "brief epic" with a philosophic theme; this type of poem, especially with an Old Testa-

83

ment or similarly "exotic" background, was to be highly important in the nineteenth century.

The posthumous volume *Les Destinées* (1864) contains only eleven poems (written after the 1837 edition of *Poèmes antiques et modernes*), but these include his best: "La Mort du loup" (The Death of the Wolf); "La Bouteille à la mer" (The Bottle in the Sea), in which the discoveries of a doomed explorer are transmitted to posterity by the symbolic floating bottle; "La Colère de Samson" (Samson's Wrath), a bitter indictment of woman's eternal treachery; "L'Esprit pur" (Pure Spirit), which glorifies the poet's art above all other kinds of nobility; and "La Maison du berger" (The Shepherd's House, first published in the *Revue des Deux Mondes* in July 1844), a section of which is given here. Addressing "Éva" (an inscrutable composite of all that is best in woman), the poet invites her to abandon the empty noise of the city and other modern horrors (the poem includes a strong attack on railroads) for the blessings of the country; the "shepherd's

La Maison du Berger (*extrait*)

Éva, j'aimerai tout dans les choses créées,
Je les contemplerai dans ton regard rêveur
Qui partout répandra ses flammes colorées,
Son repos gracieux, sa magique saveur:
Sur mon cœur déchiré viens poser ta main pure,
Ne me laisse jamais seul avec la Nature,
Car je la connais trop pour n'en pas avoir peur.

Elle me dit: "Je suis l'impassible théâtre
Que ne peut remuer le pied de ses acteurs;
Mes marches d'émeraude et mes parvis d'albâtre,
Mes colonnes de marbre ont les dieux pour sculpteurs.
Je n'entends ni vos cris ni vos soupirs; à peine
Je sens passer sur moi la comédie humaine
Qui cherche en vain au ciel ses muets spectateurs,

house," a hut on wheels used as a dwelling by shepherds, becomes the symbol of a free, roaming existence. But although Nature is beautiful, she is impersonal, and only a rich human relationship (and the grace of poetry) can make life tolerable.

Besides the works already mentioned, Vigny's production includes the influential historical novel *Cinq-Mars* (1826), adaptations of Shakespearean plays, and several original dramas (especially *Chatterton*, 1835). The poet was elected to the Académie Française in 1845 after years of fruitless solicitations on his part. After 1848 Vigny became interested in politics, but was never able to become a Deputy. He spent a great part of his later years at his country home, writing and caring for his ailing wife. The term "ivory tower" (*tour d'ivoire*) was coined by the critic Sainte-Beuve with regard to Vigny's withdrawal, but scholars have recently emphasized the poet's continuing interest in worthy causes and the careers of young writers.

The Shepherd's House (excerpt)

Eva, I shall love each one of the created things,
I shall contemplate them in your dreamy glance,
Which will spread everywhere its brightly colored flames,
Its graceful repose, its magical savor:
Come place your pure hand on my tattered heart;
Never leave me alone with Nature,
For I know her too well not to be afraid of her.

She tells me: "I am the impassive theater
Which cannot be moved by the feet of its actors;
My emerald steps and my alabaster courts,
My marble columns were sculptured by the gods.
I hear neither your shouts nor your sighs; I barely
Feel passing over me the human comedy
That futilely seeks its mute spectators in the sky;

"Je roule avec dédain, sans voir et sans entendre,
A côté des fourmis les populations;
Je ne distingue pas leur terrier de leur cendre,
J'ignore en les portant les noms des nations.
On me dit une mère et je suis une tombe.
Mon hiver prend vos morts comme son hécatombe,
Mon printemps ne sent pas vos adorations.

"Avant vous, j'étais belle et toujours parfumée,
J'abandonnais au vent mes cheveux tout entiers,
Je suivais dans les cieux ma route accoutumée
Sur l'axe harmonieux des divins balanciers.
Après vous, traversant l'espace où tout s'élance,
J'irai seule et sereine, en un chaste silence
Je fendrai l'air du front et de mes seins altiers."

C'est là ce que me dit sa voix triste et superbe,
Et dans mon cœur alors je la hais, et je vois
Notre sang dans son onde et nos morts sous son herbe
Nourrissant de leurs sucs la racine des bois.
Et je dis à mes yeux qui lui trouvaient des charmes:
"Ailleurs tous vos regards, ailleurs toutes vos larmes,
Aimez ce que jamais on ne verra deux fois."

Disdainfully, unseeing and unhearing, I roll
Human populations alongside of ants;
I do not distinguish their burrow from their ashes;
Though I bear them, I do not know the names of the nations.
I am called a mother and I am a tomb.
My winter takes your dead as its hecatomb,
My spring does not perceive your adorations.

Before your time, I was beautiful and always perfumed;
I let my hair float at full length in the wind;
I followed my customary route in the heavens
On the harmonious axle of the divine balance-wheels.
After your time, crossing space where all things fling themselves,
I shall proceed alone and serene; in chaste silence
I shall cleave the air with my brow and my haughty breasts."

That is what her sad and proud voice says to me,
And in my heart then I hate her, and I see
Our blood in her waves and our dead beneath her grass
Nourishing with their juices the root of the woods.
And I tell my eyes, which found her charming:
"Let all your glances go elsewhere, all your tears elsewhere,
Love that which will never be seen twice."

VICTOR HUGO

Born in Besançon, 1802; died in Paris, 1885

HUGO stands alone in the history of French literature. His prose and verse plays were the most important of the Romantic age; his novels constitute a titanic achievement in themselves, while his other prose works are of considerable beauty and significance. His biography is of extreme interest. All that can be offered here, however, is a pitifully brief sketch of his poetic production, which alone fills a large and crowded volume of over 1700 pages. Many important poetic fragments were published for the first time as recently as 1951, and undoubtedly more new revelations can be expected. This output (of which only certain elements are popularly known and appreciated) is so vast and varied that even some eminent scholars find it convenient to discredit or disregard large parts of it (pre- or post-exile works). Those who have occupied themselves with the entire *œuvre* have been rewarded with the discovery of a consistent development, which not only is a *summa* of nineteenth-century thought and aspirations but also contains numerous unique and exciting aspects.

The young Hugo's *Odes* appeared in 1822, the year of his marriage. After successive enlarged editions, the collection finally became the *Odes et Ballades* of 1828. The odes are noble, in the vein of Malherbe, and are largely on rather conventional political subjects; the ballads are based not on the old French *ballade*, but on the Romantic German and English ballads. The volume also contains reminiscences of Hugo's travels in Spain and Italy in the company of his father, a Napoleonic general.

The *Orientales* of 1829, written in a variety of forms, introduces the exotic colors of modern Greece and the Near East. Famous poems of this collection are the "Adieux de l'hôtesse arabe" (Farewell of the Arabian Hostess) and the virtuoso, onomato-poetic "Les Djinns."

Les Feuilles d'automne (Autumn Leaves, 1831) contains poems on ethical and cosmological problems, appreciations of childhood, the necessity of social charity, the grandeur of nature and other themes. Hugo's technical skill grows with each new volume.

Les Chants du crépuscule (Songs of Twilight, 1835) includes political poems of renewed vigor and reflections of the poet's love for his mistress Juliette Drouet (faithful to him from 1833 until her death fifty years later).

Les Voix intérieures (Inner Voices, 1837) and *Les Rayons et les ombres* (Beams and Shadows, 1840) add splendid new poems on many of Hugo's old themes. The gem of the latter collection is "Tristesse d'Olympio," a lament on the passage of time and youthful happiness. The first selection below, "Nuits de juin" (June Nights), from this same volume, is one of Hugo's brief but perceptive atmospheric word-paintings.

Hugo continued writing poetry, but did not publish any more for thirteen years. Uppermost in his mind during this period were his political activities (election to the Académie, 1841; nomination as a Peer, 1845; election as Deputy, 1848 and 1849), which were brought to an abrupt halt in 1851, when the poet was banished for his opposition to the *coup d'état* of Louis-Napoléon. His exile began in Belgium and continued in the Channel Islands of Jersey (1852–55) and Guernsey (1855–70, his exile being voluntary from 1859 on).

It is the poetry of Hugo's exile that is most esteemed today. In 1853 he published *Châtiments* (Punishments), which contains paeans to liberty and violent satirical attacks on Napoleon III, the most famous being "L'Expiation," which reviews the many sorrows of Napoleon I and concludes that the direst is his glorification by his unworthy descendant.

Les Contemplations (1856) is probably Hugo's strongest volume. The emotion that dominates the entire book is the poet's grief for the death of his daughter Léopoldine, who drowned in the Seine at Villequier (near Le Havre) in 1843. The second selection in-cluded here (written in 1847, before the exile), "Demain, dès l'aube . . ." (Tomorrow, at the point of dawn . . .), commemorates this loss. But *Les Contemplations* also contains literary polemics, nature studies (especially of the sea), amorous poetry and large-scale metaphysical disquisitions, chief of which is "Ce que dit la Bouche d'ombre" (What the Mouth of Shadow Says).

Hugo's largest collection, which appeared in three series (1859, 1877, 1883), is *La Légende des siècles* (The Legend of the Ages), a group of "short epics" illustrating the development of humanity and social consciousness throughout history. The merits of the volume are too numerous for individual mention; the biblical section alone includes "La Conscience" (on Cain's remorse) and "Booz endormi" (Boaz Sleeping).

Les Chansons des rues et des bois (Songs of Streets and Woods, 1865) are light, often erotic, lyrics whose frothy spirit and bold versification are harbingers of Verlaine's best work.

Hugo was back in France during the Franco-Prussian War; *L'Année terrible* (The Terrible Year; 1872) is a poetic journal of those trying days, rendered even harder for Hugo by the death of his son Charles in 1871.

The poet's love for children, and especially his own grandchildren, received its fullest expression in the 1877 volume *L'Art d'être grand-père* (The Art of Being a Grandfather).

The following years saw the publication of several long didactic and polemic poems: *Le Pape* (The Pope) in 1878; *La Pitié suprême* in 1879; *Religions et religion* and *L'Âne* (The Ass) in 1880.

Les quatre Vents de l'Esprit (The Four Winds of the Spirit, 1881) contains a selection of satires, verse playlets, short lyrics and other pieces.

Posthumous publications include *La Fin de Satan* (The End of Satan, 1886) and *Dieu* (God, 1891), huge unfinished philosophic works with sections of great power; *Toute la Lyre* (1888, 1893), a varied volume that contains the aged poet's tribute to the memory of his friend Théophile Gautier; *Les Années funestes* (The Baleful Years; 1898); *Dernier Gerbe* (Last Sheaf, 1902); and a multitude of fragments published in 1942 and 1951.

Nuits de juin

L'été, lorsque le jour a fui, de fleurs couverte
La plaine verse au loin un parfum enivrant;
Les yeux fermés, l'oreille aux rumeurs entrouverte,
On ne dort qu'à demi d'un sommeil transparent.

Les astres sont plus purs, l'ombre paraît meilleure;
Un vague demi-jour teint le dôme éternel;
Et l'aube douce et pâle, en attendant son heure,
Semble toute la nuit errer au bas du ciel.

"Demain, dès l'aube, à l'heure où blanchit la campagne"

Demain, dès l'aube, à l'heure où blanchit la campagne,
Je partirai. Vois-tu, je sais que tu m'attends.
J'irai par la forêt, j'irai par la montagne.
Je ne puis demeurer loin de toi plus longtemps.

Je marcherai les yeux fixés sur mes pensées,
Sans rien voir au dehors, sans entendre aucun bruit,
Seul, inconnu, le dos courbé, les mains croisées,
Triste, et le jour pour moi sera comme la nuit.

Je ne regarderai ni l'or du soir qui tombe,
Ni les voiles au loin descendant vers Harfleur,
Et quand j'arriverai, je mettrai sur ta tombe
Un bouquet de houx vert et de bruyère en fleur.

VICTOR HUGO

June Nights

In summer, when day has fled, the plain covered with flowers
Pours out an intoxicating perfume far off;
With closed eyes, with ears partially open to sounds,
One only half-sleeps with a transparent slumber.

The stars are purer, the darkness more inviting;
A vague half-light tints the eternal dome;
And the sweet and pale dawn, awaiting its time,
Seems to be wandering low in the sky all night.

"Tomorrow, at the point of dawn, at the hour when the countryside grows white"

Tomorrow, at the point of dawn, at the hour when the
    countryside grows white,
I shall depart. You see, I know you are expecting me.
I shall go through the forest, I shall go over the mountain.
I cannot remain far from you any longer.

I shall walk with my eyes fixed upon my thoughts,
Seeing nothing outside, hearing no noise,
Alone, unknown, my back stooped, my hands crossed,
Sad, and the day will be like night for me.

I shall not look at the gold of evening falling,
Nor at the sails in the distance going down toward Harfleur,
And when I arrive, I shall place on your tomb
A bouquet of green holly and flowering briar.

GÉRARD DE NERVAL

Born in Paris, 1808; died there, 1855

G ÉRARD LABRUNIE (later to call himself de Nerval after the name of a family property) lived until he was six with an uncle in a rural area of Île-de-France to which he often returned for nostalgic vacations. When his father (an Army doctor whose wife had accompanied him to the field and had died in Germany) returned from the Emperor's service, Gérard was sent to school in Paris; Théophile Gautier was his classmate. Like Gautier, Nerval was among the youthful partisans of Hugo in the literary wars of Romanticism. His earliest work comprised journalism, plays, poetry, free translations of German poems (especially the first part of *Faust*, 1828, the second part not being completed until 1840) and tales in the spirit of Hoffmann. Between 1834 and 1836 he squandered a large inheritance on riotous living and an unsuccessful magazine, and was constantly in debt from then on. Journalism became a necessity; all Nerval's later books were compiled from magazine installments he had written previously. His life became an alternating pattern of traveling to gather copy for articles and the subsequent completion of the articles. He also collaborated with Alexandre Dumas *père* in several stage works.

In 1841 Nerval suffered the first of many fits of madness. Even in his lengthy periods of lucidity and hard work he continued to elaborate and cherish a personal mythology in which fanciful genealogies, occult lore and his idealization of his mother, as well as memories of old homes and old sweethearts, played a large part. The major opus of his maturity was the *Voyage en Orient* (published in book form 1851), based on his 1842–43 trip to Egypt and Syria. *Les Filles du feu* (The Fire Maidens, 1854) contains the novella "Sylvie," often considered his masterpiece. *Aurélia* (1855)

95

is a clearly written and carefully constructed account of Nerval's fearful dream world. He was found hanged in a Paris alley on January 26, 1855. The large prose output of his later years included significant examples of all the genres for which he had been known in his youth.

In striking contrast to Hugo, Nerval owes his importance in the history of French poetry to a handful of pieces. Disregarding his completely forgotten political and satirical juvenilia, his total poetic production is very slender, and most of this is promising or charming rather than great. But Nerval cast a unique and lasting spell with the *Chimères*, a group of twelve sonnets published in their final form in 1854 along with *Les Filles du feu* (they had been published earlier, with variations, several times—"Delfica," the fifth sonnet in the 1854 grouping, included here, had originally

Delfica

La connais-tu, Dafné, cette ancienne romance,
Au pied du sycomore, ou sous les lauriers blancs,
Sous l'olivier, le myrte, ou les saules tremblants,
Cette chanson d'amour qui toujours recommence? . . .

Reconnais-tu le TEMPLE au péristyle immense,
Et les citrons amers où s'imprimaient tes dents,
Et la grotte, fatale aux hôtes imprudents,
Où du dragon vaincu dort l'antique semence? . . .

Ils reviendront, ces Dieux que tu pleures toujours!
Le temps va ramener l'ordre des anciens jours;
La terre a tressailli d'un souffle prophétique . . .

Cependant la sibylle au visage latin
Est endormie encor sous l'arc de Constantin
— Et rien n'a dérangé le sévère portique.

appeared in the magazine *L'Artiste* in December 1845). These often obscure sonnets (the subject of numerous commentaries) are the supreme distillation of the poet's reveries and hopes. Their strange verbal beauty is of immediate potency and can be satisfying without annotations; readers who wish to explore their content further must consult the other works by Nerval associated with them.

"Delfica" shows the blending of many elements. It is basically a souvenir of the poet's Italian journey (compare the novella "Octavie" in *Les Filles du feu*), filtered through Mignon's famous song "Kennst du das Land" in Goethe's *Wilhelm Meister*, and colored by Nerval's expectation of the resurgence of an enlightened paganism that would not destroy, but subsume, the ethos of Christianity.

Delfica

Do you know it, Daphne, that old romance,
At the foot of the sycamore or beneath the white laurels,
Beneath the olive tree, the myrtle, or the trembling willows,
That song of love constantly recommencing? . . .

Do you recognize the Temple with the vast peristyle,
And the bitter lemons in which your teeth left their mark,
And the grotto, fatal to heedless visitors,
Where the ancient seed of the conquered dragon sleeps? . . .

They shall return, those Gods you always lament!
Time will bring back the order of olden days;
The earth has shuddered with a gust of prophecy . . .

Meanwhile the Sibyl with the Latin face
Is still asleep beneath the Arch of Constantine
— And nothing has disturbed the severe portico.

ALFRED DE MUSSET

Born in Paris, 1810; died there, 1857

O F noble birth but without fortune, Musset tried his hand at law, medicine, music and painting before responding fully to his poetic vocation. Such was the precocity of his talent that in 1828 he was admitted as a peer to the literary circle of Hugo, Vigny and Sainte-Beuve, all older men. Yet he very shortly became an independent, shunning political ambitions and mocking features of the Romantic style. Nor were the partisans of classicism pleased by Musset's life as a dandy, gamester and Don Juan or by the mischievous form and content of his earlier poems.

The *Premières Poésies* (this designation was first used in the 1852 edition of the complete poetry) includes the volumes *Contes d'Espagne et d'Italie* (Tales of Spain and Italy, 1830) and *Un Spectacle dans un fauteuil* (The Armchair Theatergoer, 1832), as well as individual poems published in periodicals up to mid-1833. Graceful songs, elegant irony, psychological finesse, amorous ardor and ready wit abound in this collection, which also contains the first statements of Musset's poetical credo: that great poetry should be emotion committed to writing while still hotly felt.

The collection *Poésies nouvelles*, comprising most of Musset's later poetry, contains a good number of light pieces, but its most interesting works are the long serious poems which reflect the conflicts between the reality of the poet's existence and his idealistic aspirations, between the claims of his art and his longing for a fully lived life crowned by a lasting love. These poems include the "Nights" ("La Nuit de mai" and "La Nuit de décembre," 1835; "La Nuit d'août," 1836; "La Nuit d'octobre," 1837) and "Souvenir" (1841), which look back to his tempestuous affair with George Sand between 1833 and 1835.

A good number of important poems were not published until after Musset's death; several others appeared in periodicals but for various reasons were not collected. Among this latter group is "Sur une Morte," included here; it was first published in the *Revue des Deux Mondes* in October 1842. The "morte" of the poem, Princess Belgiojoso, was not at all dead but coquettishly indifferent to the poet's advances; the readers of the *Revue* understood.

After 1840 Musset wrote relatively little; he had given his best between the ages of twenty and thirty. His last years were often clouded by illness. Besides poetry, his literary output includes short stories, criticism, the autobiographical novel *La Confession d'un enfant du siècle* (Confession of a Child of the Age; 1836) and above all a group of plays that now forms one of the glories of the French theater, although—or because—most of them were not written with practical production in mind. Among these prose plays are *Fantasio, On ne badine pas avec l'amour* (One Should Not Trifle with Love) and *Lorenzaccio*, all published in 1834.

From 1838 to 1848 Musset was the chief librarian of the Ministry of the Interior; in 1853 he became a librarian at the Ministry of Public Education. He was elected to the Académie Française in 1852.

Sur une Morte

Elle était belle, si la Nuit
Qui dort dans la sombre chapelle
Où Michel-Ange a fait son lit,
Immobile peut être belle.

Elle était bonne, s'il suffit
Qu'en passant la main s'ouvre et donne,
Sans que Dieu n'ait rien vu, rien dit,
Si l'or sans pitié fait l'aumône.

Elle pensait, si le vain bruit
D'une voix douce et cadencée
Comme le ruisseau qui gémit
Peut faire croire à la pensée.

Elle priait, si deux beaux yeux,
Tantôt s'attachant à la terre,
Tantôt se levant vers les cieux,
Peuvent s'appeler la Prière.

Elle aurait souri, si la fleur
Qui ne s'est point épanouie
Pouvait s'ouvrir à la fraîcheur
Du vent qui passe et qui l'oublie.

Elle aurait pleuré si sa main,
Sur son cœur froidement posée,
Eût jamais, dans l'argile humain,
Senti la céleste rosée.

Elle aurait aimé, si l'orgueil
Pareil à la lampe inutile
Qu'on allume près d'un cercueil,
N'eût veillé sur son cœur stérile.

Elle est morte, et n'a point vécu.
Elle faisait semblant de vivre.
De ses mains est tombé le livre
Dans lequel elle n'a rien lu.

On a Dead Woman

She was beautiful, if the Night
That sleeps in the somber chapel
Where Michelangelo made his bed
Can, in her immobility, be beautiful.

She was kind, if it is enough
That in passing the hand opens and gives,
Though God has seen nothing, said nothing,
If gold without pity constitutes alms.

She thought, if the empty noise
Of a sweet and cadenced voice,
Like the moaning brook,
Can be credited with thought.

She prayed, if two beautiful eyes,
Now fixing themselves on the earth,
Now raising themselves to the heavens,
Can be called Prayer.

She would have smiled, if the flower
That never unfolded
Could open to the freshness
Of the wind that passes and forgets it.

She would have wept if her hand,
Coldly poised on her heart,
Had ever, in the human clay,
Felt the celestial dew.

She would have loved, if pride,
Like the useless lamp
Which one lights near a coffin,
Had not watched over her barren heart.

She is dead, and never lived.
She pretended to live.
From her hands the book has fallen
In which she read nothing.

THÉOPHILE GAUTIER

Born in Tarbes, 1811; died at Neuilly (Paris), 1872

THÉOPHILE GAUTIER is the literary godfather of many important trends in later nineteenth-century French poetry. Both Parnassians and Symbolists profited by his emphasis on formal perfection (often disregarded by such earlier poets as Lamartine and Musset) and his taboo on the effusive personal confessions of these and other great Romantics; it was the Parnassians especially who inherited the frigidity of his "art for art's sake."

Gautier was born in the Pyrenees. Three years later his family moved to Paris, where his father became a civil servant. The poet's early art training gave him a "painter's eye" which is much in evidence in all his writings. In the early 1830's he was a staunch supporter of Hugo, but by 1833 his volume of tales and essays, *Les Jeune-France,* already indulges in anti-Romantic irony. By the mid-1830's he was completely enslaved by his lifelong occupation: writing for newspapers—chiefly art and drama reviews, and later also travel reports (on trips to Spain, Algeria, Italy, Turkey and Greece, Germany, Russia, Egypt). Despite the necessity to turn out the equivalent of thousands of pages of journalistic copy (always well written) and despite the demands of his rich social life (most of the major mid-century authors were his friends), Gautier managed to write several short stories, three important novels (*Mademoiselle de Maupin,* 1835; *Le Roman de la Momie,* 1857; *Le Capitaine Fracasse,* 1861–63), the scenarios of two ballets (one was *Giselle,* 1841) and a substantial poetic *œuvre.*

The enjoyable volume *Poésies* appeared in 1830. *Albertus* (1832), a long narrative poem, satanic and Hoffmannesque, contains many a tour de force of witty description. The poems in *La Comédie de la*

Mort (1838) show Gautier's later, less extravagant tone, but still display a pleasing variety of forms, as do those in *España* (1845), which describe the stages in the poet's tour of Spain in 1840. When the volume *Émaux et Camées* (Enamels and Cameos) was first published in 1852, it contained only eighteen pieces; later editions brought this number to forty-seven. This was to become Gautier's most famous collection.

Enamels are small and unspectacular, but require a sure touch and have a permanent baked finish; cameos are carved with great effort from very hard and very durable stone. Similarly, the poet hopes that the care he has lavished on the expression of these random thoughts and sketches will gain him immortality. All but the last three of these poems are written in octosyllabic quatrains. The exotic element sometimes becomes pedantic, and the descriptive material allegorical, but the charm of the collection is undeniable.

"Carmen," included here, which appeared first in the 1863 edition of *Émaux*, is a fine example of Gautier's wit (featuring unusual rhymes for foreign words), eroticism and sense of color. The description of the gypsy girl parallels that of the Soubrette in *Le Capitaine Fracasse*, which Gautier was working on about the same time.

Carmen

Carmen est maigre, — un trait de bistre
Cerne son œil de gitana.
Ses cheveux sont d'un noir sinistre,
Sa peau, le diable la tanna.

Les femmes disent qu'elle est laide,
Mais tous les hommes en sont fous,
Et l'archevêque de Tolède
Chante la messe à ses genoux;

Car sur sa nuque d'ambre fauve
Se tord un énorme chignon
Qui, dénoué, fait dans l'alcôve
Une mante à son corps mignon.

Et, parmi sa pâleur, éclate
Une bouche aux rires vainqueurs;
Piment rouge, fleur écarlate,
Qui prend sa pourpre au sang des cœurs.

Ainsi faite, la moricaude
Bat les plus altières beautés,
Et de ses yeux la lueur chaude
Rend la flamme aux satiétés.

Elle a, dans sa laideur piquante,
Un grain de sel de cette mer
D'où jaillit, nue et provocante,
L'âcre Vénus du gouffre amer.

Carmen

Carmen is thin—a dark ring
Circles her gypsy eyes.
Her hair is a sinister black,
Her hide was tanned by the devil.

The women say she is ugly,
But all the men are crazy for her,
And the Archbishop of Toledo
Sings Mass at her knees;

For on her nape of tawny amber
Is twisted an enormous coil of hair,
Which, when undone, in the bedroom,
Forms a cloak for her delicate body.

And amid her pallor there flashes
A mouth whose laughter conquers,
A red pepper, a scarlet flower,
That draws its purple from the blood of hearts.

With this appearance, the dark-skinned girl
Surpasses the proudest beauties,
And the warm glow of her eyes
Rekindles a flame in jaded appetites.

She possesses, in her piquant homeliness,
A grain of salt of that sea
From which issued, nude and inviting,
The acrid Venus of the bitter abyss.

CHARLES BAUDELAIRE

Born in Paris, 1821; died there, 1867

LES FLEURS DU MAL (The Flowers of Evil) is often con-
sidered to be the pivotal book in the history of modern, if
not of all, French poetry. No poet had looked more deeply into
the recesses of his personality or had conceived, simultaneously,
such pride in his inspired calling and such loathing for his human
frailties; none had expressed these feelings so cogently or with
such merciless psychological probing. Baudelaire explores the
gamut of escape mechanisms—musings on childhood, dreams,
travel, alcohol, sex seamy and sublimated, hallucinatory drugs
(discussed further in the 1860 prose work *Les Paradis artificiels*)—
but never shakes off his inherent melancholy (*spleen*), never loses
sight of his weaknesses. At the same time, he does not remain en-
closed in his malady, but extends his sympathies to the poor and
the oppressed, to the outcasts and the unwanted, all the human
flotsam he had ample opportunity to observe in his profound
experience of Parisian life.

Although the outer forms of these poems are still orthodox, *Les
Fleurs du Mal* has also had a marked influence on the techniques of
French poetry, especially because of the powerful "musicality"
of the verse and the headiness of the sensuous imagery.

When Baudelaire was six, his father died; his mother married
an army officer the next year. After school years in Lyons and
Paris, Baudelaire began to shock his parents by his extravagant
existence. In 1841 he was sent on a voyage to India, but got no
farther than the islands of Mauritius and Réunion. Back in Paris,
his profligacy led his family in 1844 to furnish him permanently
with a legal guardian. Baudelaire began to publish in 1845: a
poem and the first of several books of art criticism. The reviews of

contemporary art collected in the posthumous volumes *L'Art romantique* and *Curiosités esthétiques* (both 1869) are unusually perceptive; Baudelaire's preferences have been largely confirmed by posterity. The extensive translations of works by Poe began in 1853. During the late 1840's and the 1850's various magazines published several of the poems that were to be collected in *Les Fleurs du Mal* and some of the short prose pieces that were to form the *Petits Poëmes en prose* (1869, also known as *Le Spleen de Paris*).

The appearance of *Les Fleurs du Mal* in 1857 (dedicated to Gautier) led to a prosecution for indecency and blasphemy, a fine for Baudelaire and the suppression of six of the poems. Enlarged editions appeared in 1861 (the key edition) and 1868. Rejected by the Académie Française in 1862 and hounded by creditors,

La Vie antérieure

J'ai longtemps habité sous de vastes portiques
Que les soleils marins teignaient de mille feux,
Et que leurs grands piliers, droits et majestueux,
Rendaient pareils, le soir, aux grottes basaltiques.

Les houles, en roulant les images des cieux,
Mêlaient d'une façon solennelle et mystique
Les tout-puissants accords de leur riche musique
Aux couleurs du couchant reflété par mes yeux,

C'est là que j'ai vécu dans les voluptés calmes,
Au milieu de l'azur, des vagues, des splendeurs
Et des esclaves nus, tout imprégnés d'odeurs,

Qui me rafraîchissaient le front avec des palmes,
Et dont l'unique soin était d'approfondir
Le secret douloureux qui me faisait languir.

Baudelaire left Paris for Belgium in 1864. His lectures there were unsuccessful. In 1866 he suffered a paralytic stroke and was brought back to Paris, where he died the next year.

The sonnet "La Vie antérieure" (My Former Life) was one of eighteen poems first published in the *Revue des Deux Mondes* in 1855 and later included in *Les Fleurs du Mal* (the poem appears as number XII in all editions). It has been suggested that this particular escape-vision, embodying memories of the Indian Ocean voyage and employing many images that recur in other pieces, originates in Baudelaire's experiences with opium. "Je suis comme le roi," the third of four consecutive poems all entitled "Spleen," first appeared in the 1857 volume of *Les Fleurs*; it bears the number LXXVII in the 1861 edition.

My Former Life

For a long time I lived beneath vast porticos,
Which the ocean suns tinted with a thousand fires;
Their great pillars, straight and majestic,
Made them similar, in the evening, to basaltic grottos.

The surf, rolling the images of the skies,
In solemn and mystic fashion mingled
The all-powerful chords of its rich music
With the setting sun's colors reflected in my eyes.

It is there that I lived in calm delights,
In the midst of the azure, the waves, the splendors
And the naked slaves, thoroughly steeped in perfumes,

Who cooled my brow with palm leaves,
And whose sole concern was to penetrate
The painful secret which made me languish.

Line 13: *Approfondir*, here translated as "penetrate," may also be taken to mean "deepen."

Spleen

Je suis comme le roi d'un pays pluvieux,
Riche, mais impuissant, jeune et pourtant très vieux,
Qui, de ses précepteurs méprisant les courbettes,
S'ennuie avec ses chiens comme avec d'autres bêtes.
Rien ne peut l'égayer, ni gibier, ni faucon,
Ni son peuple mourant en face du balcon.
Du bouffon favori la grotesque ballade
Ne distrait plus le front de ce cruel malade;
Son lit fleurdelisé se transforme en tombeau,
Et les dames d'atour, pour qui tout prince est beau,
Ne savent plus trouver d'impudique toilette
Pour tirer un souris de ce jeune squelette.
Le savant qui lui fait de l'or n'a jamais pu
De son être extirper l'élément corrompu,
Et dans ces bains de sang qui des Romains nous viennent,
Et dont sur leurs vieux jours les puissants se souviennent,
Il n'a su réchauffer ce cadavre hébété
Où coule au lieu de sang l'eau verte du Léthé.

Melancholy

I am like the king of a rainy country,
Rich, but powerless, young and yet very old,
Who, scorning the bows and scrapes of his tutors,
Is bored with his dogs as with other animals.
Nothing can cheer him, neither game nor falcon,
Nor his people dying opposite his balcony.
The grotesque ballad of his favorite jester
No longer smoothes the brow of this cruel invalid;
His bed adorned with fleurs-de-lis becomes a tomb,
And the tirewomen, who find all princes handsome,
Can no longer contrive a shameless costume
That will draw a smile from this young skeleton.
The alchemist who makes gold for him has never been able
To eliminate the corrupted element from his nature,
And in those blood baths bequeathed to us by the Romans,
And which the mighty recall when they grow old,
He has not been able to restore warmth to this dulled corpse
In which, in place of blood, the green water of Lethe flows.

STÉPHANE MALLARMÉ

Born in Paris, 1842; died at Valvins near Fontainebleau, 1898

MALLARMÉ'S aim was to create a poetry of suggestion rather than description: short pieces that would be self-contained works of art, tiny universes; a small but difficult *œuvre* which would yield its beauties only to those few sufficiently dedicated and patient to confront its mysteries, some of which would linger even after the most exhaustive analyses. In pursuit of these goals, he progressively dislocated his syntax, unified his imagery, refined and limited his vocabulary, selecting fa ored words, even particular letters, and placing them where their individual "electric charges" would give the effect he desired. The result is a body of poetry often forbidding—almost demanding exegesis while simultaneously dooming it—yet of undeniable verbal beauty and fullness; often of a startling directness, the syntactic virtuosity having, for the first time in the history of French verse, freed the poetic expression from the heritage of Latin rhetoric. Even when the ostensible subjects of the poems are simple, familiar, if somewhat precious objects—a fan, a painted dish—the poet returns to his major theme: the lonely adventure of the creative spirit in a world of which nothingness is perhaps the most real element.

Born into a family of civil servants, Mallarmé (whose mother died when he was five) became a teacher of English, working from 1863 (the year of his marriage) to 1871 in various cities in the South of France, then returning to teach, until his 1894 retirement, in his native Paris. Ten of his poems were published in the first series of *Le Parnasse contemporain* in 1866. His first book (1875) contained the single poem "L'Après-midi d'un faune" (The Afternoon of a Faun), illustrated by Manet. In 1874 and 1875

Mallarmé published a highly sophisticated "fashion" magazine, *La Dernière Mode*, writing most of the columns himself under a variety of feminine pseudonyms. He inaugurated his famous social Tuesdays in 1880; for years he was a friend and mentor to a rising generation of French and foreign writers and artists: Valéry, Gide, Claudel, Oscar Wilde, Stefan George, Verhaeren, Gauguin, Whistler and many others. Verlaine's *Poètes maudits* (Accursed Poets, 1884) and Huysmans' *A Rebours* (Against the Grain, 1885) made Mallarmé's name more widely known to the public; among the initiates, he was already established as the leading voice in the group that came to be known as the Symbolists and that was to emerge as the most prominent poetic "school" by 1890. A costly small edition of Mallarmé's *Poésies* appeared in 1887; the main edition is that of 1898, which does not include his extensive

Apparition

La lune s'attristait. Des séraphins en pleurs
Rêvant, l'archet aux doigts, dans le calme des fleurs
Vaporeuses, tiraient de mourantes violes
De blancs sanglots glissant sur l'azur des corolles.
— C'était le jour béni de ton premier baiser.
Ma songerie aimant à me martyriser
S'enivrait savammant du parfum de tristesse
Que même sans regret et sans déboire laisse
La cueillaison d'un Rêve au cœur qui l'a cueilli.
J'errais donc, l'œil rivé sur le pavé vieilli
Quand avec du soleil aux cheveux, dans la rue
Et dans le soir, tu m'es en riant apparue
Et j'ai cru voir la fée au chapeau de clarté
Qui jadis sur mes beaux sommeils d'enfant gâté
Passait, laissant toujours de ses mains mal fermées
Neiger de blancs bouquets d'étoiles parfumées.

occasional verse, his important youthful poems or his unusual "typographic" poem of 1897, "Un coup de dés jamais n'abolira le hasard" (A Cast of the Dice Will Never Eliminate Chance). Mallarmé also wrote a few prose poems in the tradition of Baudelaire, critical essays, Poe translations, narratives and works on language and mythology. He died at his country home in Valvins in 1898.

The selection "Apparition" given here is a relatively early and relatively simple poem, but already unmistakably Mallarméan. It was written in 1863 and published first in Verlaine's 1884 article on Mallarmé, next in the journal *Le Scapin* in 1886 and then in the 1887 *Poésies*. It is typical of his first mature style in its melancholy, in its almost overripe sweetness and in its sexuality, all the more ardent for being indirect.

Apparition

The moon grew sad. Seraphim in tears,
Dreaming, the bow in their fingers, in the calm of the vaporous
Flowers, drew from dying viols
White sighs gliding on the azure of the corollas.
— It was the blessed day of your first kiss.
My daydream, taking pleasure in torturing me,
Became knowingly drunk on that perfume of sadness
Which even without regret and without disappointment is left
By the culling of a Dream in the heart that has culled it.
Thus I wandered, my eyes fixed on the pavement grown old,
When with sunlight in your hair, in the street
And in the evening, you appeared to me laughing
And I thought I saw the fairy with the hat of brightness
Who once would pass through my beautiful spoiled-child's
Slumbers, always letting her not-quite-closed hands
Snow down white bouquets of perfumed stars.

PAUL VERLAINE

Born in Metz, 1844; died in Paris, 1896

VERLAINE was born in Lorraine, where his father, an army officer, was stationed. The family came to Paris in 1851. After some law studies, Paul, who had started to write verse by the time he was fourteen, became a municipal clerk. His first volume of poetry, the *Poèmes saturniens* (1866), already announces the two paths his art was to take: autobiographical verse, often self-pitying in tone, quite traditional in form (chiefly in alexandrines); and poems in short lines and short stanzas, bathed in a dreamy half-light, as vague and compelling as an emotion still unchanneled by the reasoning mind. *Fêtes galantes* (1869), Verlaine's most unified volume, is completely devoted to the latter style; a muted eroticism suffuses these evocations of eighteenth-century pastoral badinage.

By this time the poet was already subject to periodic outbursts of violence, aggravated by his drinking. He married in 1870, hoping that a settled bourgeois life would cure these troubles and his homosexuality; the volume *La bonne Chanson* (The Good Song, not published until 1872) dates from the period of his courtship. Rimbaud's arrival in Paris in September 1871 was to change this outlook. In July 1872 the two poets left together for Belgium, then England. The escapade was poetically rewarding—during this period Verlaine wrote the poems of his most admired volume, *Romances sans paroles* (Songs Without Words, published 1874)—but personally hellish, ending in Brussels in July 1873, when Verlaine shot Rimbaud in the wrist. During his subsequent imprisonment, which lasted until January 1875 (his wife divorced him in 1874), Verlaine was converted to Catholicism; henceforth, Christian remorse was to be one of his abiding themes. The volume

Sagesse (Proper Conduct, 1880) contains the deeply felt poems of the period of conversion, as well as a few pieces—his last—in the "dreamy" style.

After prison, Verlaine taught in England and France (1875–79); ran a farm for three years; returned to Paris for a while; led a scandalous rural existence from 1883 to 1885; then returned to Paris, where most of his last ten years were divided between hospitals, cafés and seamy rooming houses. His later books of verse include *Jadis et naguère* (Long Ago and Recently; 1884) the (more or less) religious "series" *Amour* (Love, 1888), *Bonheur* (Happiness, 1891) and *Liturgies intimes* (1892); the erotic "series" *Parallèlement* (1889), *Chansons pour Elle* (Songs for Her, 1891), *Odes en son honneur* (Odes in Her Honor, 1893), *Élégies* (1893) and *Dans les Limbes* (In Limbo; 1894); and various other collections, some (*Femmes* and *Hombres*) outspokenly pornographic. Verlaine's glory grew as his powers rusted; by 1885 he was the recognized head of the poetic "school" known as the Decadents and was also connected with other later movements, but finished as a traditional independent. His prose works include autobiographical pieces, travel sketches, tales, prose poems and the influential

En Sourdine

Calmes dans le demi-jour
Que les branches hautes font,
Pénétrons bien notre amour
De ce silence profond.

Fondons nos âmes, nos cœurs
Et nos sens extasiés,
Parmi les vagues langueurs
Des pins et des arbousiers.

articles *Poètes maudits* (Accursed Poets, 1883 ff.), which focused public attention on Mallarmé and Rimbaud as well as on Verlaine himself.

Both poems included here are in the relatively uncommon seven-syllable meter. "En Sourdine" is the next to the last of the twenty-two *Fêtes galantes*. "L'échelonnement des haies" (poem III, XIII of *Sagesse*), written at Bournemouth in England in 1876, is a superb example of the style that is uniquely, most inimitably Verlainian. The thorough blending in the imagination of all the elements of the landscape (the white-blooming hedgerows, the sea foam, the sheep, the milky sky) is matched by an uncanny (and quite untranslatable) blending of sound and sense. Among the numerous verbal felicities of these summer-drenched lines, with their insidious network of internal rhymes, one may note the verb "moutonne" (line 2), which means "breaks into foam" (here translated reluctantly as "billows" for brevity), but which contains the word "mouton" (sheep) within it; and the masculine noun "vague" (line 9)—itself participating in the vagueness of a substantivized adjective—which irresistibly conjures up the feminine noun "vague"—a wave!

Muted

Calm in the half-daylight
That the high branches create,
Let us thoroughly steep our love
In this deep silence.

Let us fuse our souls, our hearts
And our enraptured senses
Amid the vague languors
Of the pines and the arbutus.

Ferme tes yeux à demi,
Croise tes bras sur ton sein,
Et de ton cœur endormi
Chasse à jamais tout dessein.

Laissons-nous persuader
Au souffle berceur et doux
Qui vient à tes pieds rider
Les ondes de gazon roux.

Et quand, solennel, le soir
Des chênes noirs tombera,
Voix de notre désespoir,
Le rossignol chantera.

"L'échelonnement des haies"

L'échelonnement des haies
Moutonne à l'infini, mer
Claire dans le brouillard clair
Qui sent bon les jeunes baies.

Des arbres et des moulins
Sont légers sur le vert tendre
Où vient s'ébattre et s'étendre
L'agilité des poulains.

Dans ce vague d'un Dimanche
Voici se jouer aussi
De grandes brebis aussi
Douces que leur laine blanche.

Tout à l'heure déferlait
L'onde, roulée en volutes,
De cloches comme des flûtes
Dans le ciel comme du lait.

Half-close your eyes,
Cross your arms on your breast,
And from your sleeping heart
Drive away all purpose forever.

Let us abandon ourselves
To the rocking and gentle breeze
That comes and at your feet wrinkles
The waves of auburn grass.

And when, solemnly, the evening
Falls from the black oaks,
Voice of our despair,
The nightingale will sing.

"The gradation of the hedges"

The gradation of the hedges
Billows to infinity, a sea
Bright in the bright fog
With its good smell of young berries.

Trees and mills
Are weightless on the tender green
Where the agility of the colts
Comes to sport and lie down.

In this Sunday vagueness,
Here there are, also frolicking,
Large sheep as
Gentle as their white wool.

A moment ago there broke
The wave, rolled in volutes,
Of flute-like bells
In the milk-like sky.

ARTHUR RIMBAUD

Born in Charleville, 1854; died in Marseilles, 1891

A PRECOCIOUS child tyrannized by his mother (his father, an army captain, rarely lingered at home between 1855 and 1864 and never after that) and impatient of the routine of a small town in the Ardennes, Rimbaud started writing early. By 1870, a year in which he ran away from home twice, he was already producing major poems in a personal style. His works of 1870 are fresh and optimistic, alive to the beauties of nature. Some pieces express great sympathy with the working class. The mordantly satirical poems written in the first months of 1871 (Rimbaud ran off to Paris again in February) show his increasing dissatisfaction with life in Charleville. In his letters written between May and August, he tries to arrange a permanent move to Paris and at the same time begins to formulate his poetic credo (especially in the May 15 "Letter of the Seer"): a renovation of poetic form and technique that will permit the poet-seer to be the true arbiter of the modern world. Rimbaud's poetic production of these same months culminates in "Le Bateau ivre" (The Drunken Boat), an intense, quasi-mystical development of Baudelaire's ship/sea/travel/novelty/ unknown theme-complex.

Rimbaud finally "arrived" in Paris in September 1871, at Verlaine's invitation. The two poets became inseparable companions, to the detriment of Verlaine's marriage. After Bohemian months of absinthe and hashish, the pair left (July 1872) for Belgium and England. During this period Rimbaud was working on the *Illuminations* (which possibly were not completed until 1875); this title is thought to be the English term, the sense being "manuscript illuminations" (*enluminures* in French). These short prose poems, of an imaginative form and coruscating finish new in French literature, are based on childhood recollections, scenes of travel in Belgium and England and purely imaginary visions and parables. They are presented as a series of enigmas to which the key is withheld.

By 1873 Rimbaud was writing *Une Saison en Enfer* (A Season in Hell). He finished it in France after the stormy end of his affair with Verlaine in July; it was printed, but not distributed, at the end of 1873. This poetic prose work, with its veiled allusions to the poet's experiences, is Rimbaud's formal farewell to poetry, an art which had not enabled him to "change life" or "reinvent love." From now on, he writes, he must "embrace rugged reality." After 1875 (at the latest) he wrote no more creative literature and took no active interest in the fate of what he had already written. Piecemeal publication (by others) of his works did not begin until 1886.

Between 1874 and 1878 Rimbaud unsuccessfully sought work in England, Germany, Italy, Denmark, Sweden and Egypt; a short stay in the Dutch colonial army even brought him to Java (1876). From 1878 to 1880 he worked in a Cyprus quarry. From late 1880 to early 1891 he was a trader, and to some extent an explorer, in areas of what is now eastern Ethiopia. In the spring of 1891 he returned to France, crippled by a tumor on the right knee. Amputation failed to arrest the course of his ailment, and he died in a Marseilles hospital in November of that year.

The sonnet "Ma Bohème" (My Bohemia) was written during Rimbaud's second flight from home, in the fall of 1870; it is an early, untroubled work. "Départ" (Departure), from the *Illuminations*, restates the theme of Baudelaire's "Le Voyage" (*trouver du nouveau!*—to find something new!) and of Rimbaud's own traditional-form poem "Le Bateau ivre." Now, however, in accordance with the new poetic, it delivers its message in short bursts of light: a succinct, but monumental, unforgettable expression of the poet's eternal restlessness.

Ma Bohème
(Fantaisie)

Je m'en allais, les poings dans mes poches crevées;
Mon paletot aussi devenait idéal;
J'allais sous le ciel, Muse! et j'étais ton féal;
Oh! là là! que d'amours splendides j'ai rêvées!

Mon unique culotte avait un large trou.
— Petit Poucet rêveur, j'égrenais dans ma course
Des rimes. Mon auberge était à la Grande-Ourse.
— Mes étoiles au ciel avaient un doux frou-frou

Et je les écoutais, assis au bord des routes,
Ces bons soirs de septembre où je sentais des gouttes
De rosée à mon front, comme un vin de vigueur;

Où, rimant au milieu des ombres fantastiques,
Comme des lyres, je tirais les élastiques
De mes souliers blessés, un pied près de mon cœur!

Départ

Assez vu. La vision s'est rencontrée à tous les airs.
Assez eu. Rumeurs des villes, le soir, et au soleil, et toujours.
Assez connu. Les arrêts de la vie. — O Rumeurs et Visions!
Départ dans l'affection et le bruit neufs!

My Bohemia
(Fantasy)

I went off, my fists in my torn pockets;
My overcoat, too, became ideal;
I walked beneath the sky, Muse! and I was your liege;
Oh ho! what splendid love affairs I dreamed of!

My only pair of trousers had a wide hole.
— A daydreaming Hop o' My Thumb, I strung out rhymes
As I went along. My inn was on the Big Dipper.
— My stars in the sky had a sweet rustling

And I listened to them, as I sat by the roadsides,
Those good September evenings when I felt drops
Of dew on my forehead like a heady wine;

When, rhyming amid the fantastic shadows,
Like lyres I pulled the elastic bands
Of my wounded shoes, a foot close to my heart!

Departure

Enough seen. The vision was met with in every clime.
Enough had. Sounds of cities, in the evening, and in the sun,
*   and always.*
Enough known. The decrees of life. — O Sounds and Visions!
Departure in new affection and new noise!

PAUL CLAUDEL

Born at Villeneuve-sur-Fère-en-Tardenois, 1868; died in Paris, 1955

CLAUDEL'S masterpieces of poetry and poetic drama were written during the long and active course of his diplomatic career. Born in a small village near Château-Thierry and Reims, the son of a civil servant, he had come to Paris with his family in 1881. In 1893–94 Claudel filled consular posts in New York and Boston. He spent most of the years 1895–1908 in China. Then came Prague, Frankfurt and Hamburg (to 1914), Rome (1915–16), Rio (1917–18, Copenhagen (1919–21). He was France's ambassador to Japan from 1921 to 1926; to the United States from 1927 to 1933; to Belgium until 1935, the year of his retirement. He was elected to the Académie Française in 1946.

The (published) poems—in alexandrines—Claudel wrote up to 1895, *Premiers Vers* (First Verses) and *Vers d'exil* (Verses of Exile), are already marked by his 1886 discovery of Rimbaud and his conversion to Catholicism in the same year. The descriptive and contemplative prose poems that form the volume *Connaissance de l'Est* (Acquaintance with the East) were written between 1895 and 1905. The *Cinq Grandes Odes* (Five Great Odes), written between 1900 and 1908, are composed in the sweeping lines of irregular length and rhythm that are the hallmark of the poetry of Claudel's maturity. These long odes are the lyrical transmutation of the most critical events in the poet's life; they express the conflict between the claims of poetry and those of religion, between human egoism and submission to God; they record Claudel's thwarted priestly vocation, his adulterous love affair— which is also the subject of his play *Partage de midi* (Division at Noon, 1906)—and the repose he finally found in marriage and paternity and in the conscious acceptance of Roman Catholicism.

Published along with the *Odes* (1910) was the 1907 poem "Processional pour saluer le siècle nouveau" (Processional to Greet the New Century), the first of the many Claudel poems that add rhyme (most often by couplets, but also in a variety of stanzas) to the lines of irregular length (based on natural fluctuations in exhalation and speech emission), forming the typical Psalm-like Claudelian "*versets*" (a term actually denoting Bible verses).

In 1911 Claudel wrote the exquisite *Cantate à trois voix* (Cantata for Three Voices). His other major collections of poetry are the *Corona benignitatis anni Dei* (The Crown of Benevolence of God's Year; 1915), a sequence of poems for the Christian year; *La Messe là-bas* (The Mass Yonder, 1919), written in Rio during the First World War; and *Feuilles de Saints* (Images of Saints, 1925). Other aspects of his poetic production include short pieces inspired by Japanese and Chinese poems, and translations from Aeschylus and Coventry Patmore. Claudel also published essays, a voluminous correspondence (with Gide and others) and biblical exegeses, but his greatest achievements (along with the *Odes*) are his plays, among which are *L'Annonce faite à Marie* (The Annunciation to Mary, 1912), *Le Soulier de satin* (The Satin Slipper, 1930) and *Le Livre de Christophe Colomb* (The Book of Christopher Columbus, 1935).

Claudel's best work is characterized by a rhythmic flow and by startling and profound associations of images. His unusual command of language permits easy transitions from the everyday to the elevated and, together with his vast culture and personal experience of many parts of the world, allows him to recreate poetically in breadth and depth the catholicity to which his religion aspires.

"Préface," the poem included here, was written in May 1921 (in France, between the poet's return from Denmark and his departure for Japan) as a foreword to *Morceaux choisis* (Selected Pieces), an anthology of Claudel's writings published in that year. A typical trait of such consciously "popular" poems in *versets* is the lack of regard for "masculine" as opposed to "feminine" endings in the rhyming words (for example, "luire" rhymes with "souffrir" and "mer" with "arrière").

Préface

Derrière moi la plaine, comme jadis en Chine quand je montais l'été vers Kouliang.

Le pays aplati par la distance et cette carte où l'on ne voit rien tant que l'on marche dedans,

Le chemin qu'il a fallu faire avec tant de peine et de sueur de ce point jusqu'à un autre point,

Tant de kilomètres et d'années que l'on couvrirait maintenant avec la main !

Le soleil d'un brusque rayon çà et là fait revivre et luire

Un fleuve dont on ne sait plus le nom, telle ville comme une vieille blessure qui fait encore souffrir !

Là-bas la fumée d'un paquebot qui part et la clarté spéciale que fait la mer, —

L'exil à plein cœur accepté dont nous ne sortirons qu'en avant et non pas en arrière !

Le soir tombe, considère ce site nouveau, explorateur !

Ce silence à d'autres étonnant, qu'il est familier à ton cœur !

Les montagnes l'une sur l'autre se dressent dans une attention immense.

Il faut beaucoup d'espace pour que la vie commence,

Pour que le souffle du large soit arrêté et que les eaux en ce cirque déchiré soient recueillies !

J'écoute le bruit qu'elles font et le soupir de tous ces villages sous moi dans le sucre et dans le riz.

Ma maison que j'ai abandonnée pour toujours, je n'ai qu'à me retourner pour savoir qu'elle est là-bas.

(J'entends le vent, pendant que je lis les Psaumes, qui fait remuer les stores de la vérandah.)

Je sais que tout est fini derrière moi et que le retour est exclu.

Donne avec un profond tressaillement, mon âme, dans ce pays complètement inconnu !

Pourquoi tarder plus longtemps sur ce seuil préparateur ?

Viens, si le nom d'un Père a pour toi quelque douceur.

Preface

Behind me the plain, as once in China when I would ascend in summer toward Kouliang.

The countryside flattened by the distance and that map on which you see nothing as long as you are walking within it,

The road you had to travel with so much trouble and sweat from one point up to another point,

So many miles and years which you could now cover up with your hand!

The sun with a brusque ray here and there restores life and glow

To a river whose name you no longer know, such-and-such a city like an old wound that still causes suffering!

Over there the smoke of a departing steamer and the special brightness the sea makes—

The wholeheartedly accepted exile which we shall only leave facing forward and not backward!

Evening falls; examine this new site, explorer!

This silence surprising to others, how familiar it is to your heart!

The mountains erect themselves one upon the other in an immense state of attention.

Much space is necessary for life to commence,

For the wind from the open sea to be halted and the waters to be gathered in this ragged amphitheater!

I listen to the noise the waters make and the sigh of all those villages below me in the sugar and the rice.

My house, which I have abandoned for always—I have only to turn around to know that it is over yonder.

(I hear the wind, while I read the Psalms, agitating the blinds of the veranda.)

I know that all is finished behind me and that return is out of the question.

Forward with a deep shudder, my soul, into this completely unknown country!

Why tarry longer on this preparatory threshold?

Come, if the name of a Father has any sweetness for you.

PAUL VALÉRY

Born in Sète (Cette), 1871; died in Paris, 1945

VALÉRY'S writings, of which his poetry forms a small but choice part, comprise a tireless investigation into the nature and uses of the intelligence. His youthful essays *Introduction à la Méthode de Léonard de Vinci* (1895) and *La Soirée avec M. Teste* (The Evening with Mr. Teste; 1896) announce the program for his life and art: the systematic assimilation and cross-fertilization of many areas of knowledge, avoiding the dangers of specialization and firmly disavowing the intervention of inspiration. Through a long, busy lifetime, numerous essays, prefaces, notebooks and lectures, in clear, elegant prose, on a wide array of humanistic and scientific subjects, testify to the author's strength of purpose. Skepticism and pessimism are keynotes of Valéry's thought, but he strives to avoid dogmatism. Among his most celebrated prose works are the Socratic dialogues *L'Âme et la Danse* (The Soul and the Dance) and *Eupalinos ou l'Architecte* (both 1923), the political reflections *Regards sur le Monde actuel* (Viewing the Present-day World; 1931) and *Degas, Danse, Dessin* (Degas, Dance, Drawing; 1937).

In his poetry, Valéry is the chief successor of Mallarmé, continuing the Symbolist esthetic of polished traditional form, artifice and musicality, difficult syntax and an unusual choice of words, which are often employed in their etymological sense. He makes important personal use of classical mythology. For Valéry, Narcissus is the symbol of the ego contemplating itself, while Orpheus and Amphion represent the poet who constructs works of beauty and utility from the disparate elements of language. Moreover, a rich vein of emotion, often erotic, runs through Valéry's poetry and saves it from aridity and preciosity.

The *Album de vers anciens* (Album of Early Verses), published in
1920, is a revised selection of poems that appeared in magazines
during the last decade of the nineteenth century. Valéry, born in
the Mediterranean town of Sète (then spelled Cette) in 1871—his
parents were both of Italian extraction, his father a customs
official—had met Gide and Pierre Louÿs while at the University of
Montpellier, had arrived in Paris in 1891, had attended Mallarmé's
"Tuesdays," had begun to publish and to win acclaim—then had
kept silence for twenty years, while he perfected his method and
enriched his art. Meanwhile he had married, in 1900, the same
year in which he became the private secretary of the director of
an important news service.

Valéry broke his silence with the long poem *La Jeune Parque*
(The Young Fate), a highly complex word-picture of shifting
mental states, which appeared in 1917 and almost immediately
established the poet's reputation. "Le Cimetière Marin" (The
Cemetery by the Sea, 1920), possibly his finest poem, is a sad but
resigned contemplation of mortality. It was later included in the

L'Abeille

à Francis de Miomandre

Quelle, et si fine, et si mortelle,
Que soit ta pointe, blonde abeille,
Je n'ai, sur ma tendre corbeille,
Jeté qu'un songe de dentelle.

Pique du sein la gourde belle,
Sur qui l'Amour meurt ou sommeille,
Qu'un peu de moi-même vermeille
Vienne à la chair ronde et rebelle!

collection *Charmes* (Charms—Incantations, but with the additional connotation of *carmina*, a Latin designation of lyric poetry), which first appeared in 1922 and contained the shorter works written since 1917. After 1922 Valéry wrote very little poetry, and none of great importance.

In 1927 Valéry entered the Académie Française. In 1933 he became administrator of the Centre Universitaire Méditerranéen. Four years later he was appointed to a professorship in poetics at the Collège de France. His importance in the European intellectual community was outstanding. When he died in 1945, he was buried with national honors.

The octosyllabic sonnets "L'Abeille" (The Bee) and "Le Vin perdu" (The Lost Wine) are two of the simpler and more immediately appealing poems from the volume *Charmes*. "L'Abeille," in which the poet—as he does frequently—speaks in the person of a young girl, was originally published in the *Nouvelle Revue Française* in December 1919; "Le Vin perdu" in *les feuilles libres* in February 1922.

The Bee

To Francis de Miomandre

Whatever, and howsoever sharp, and howsoever mortal
May be your point, blond bee,
I have cast over my tender basket
Only a dream of lace.

Sting the lovely gourd of the breast,
On which Love dies or slumbers,
Let a bit of my vermilion self
Rise to the round and stubborn flesh!

J'ai grand besoin d'un prompt tourment :
Un mal vif et bien terminé
Vaut mieux qu'un supplice dormant !

Soit donc mon sens illuminé
Par cette infime alerte d'or
Sans qui l'Amour meurt ou s'endort !

Le Vin perdu

J'ai, quelque jour, dans l'Océan,
(Mais je ne sais plus sous quels cieux)
Jeté, comme offrande au néant,
Tout un peu de vin précieux...

Qui voulut ta perte, ô liqueur ?
J'obéis peut-être au devin ?
Peut-être au souci de mon cœur,
Songeant au sang, versant le vin ?

Sa transparence accoutumée
Après une rose fumée
Reprit aussi pure la mer...

Perdu ce vin, ivres les ondes !...
J'ai vu bondir dans l'air amer
Les figures les plus profondes...

I have great need of a prompt torment:
A pain that smarts and ends once for all
Is better than a dormant torture!

So let my sense be illuminated
By that tiny golden alarm
Without which Love dies or drops into slumber!

The Lost Wine

One day, into the Ocean
(But I no longer know in what region)
I threw, as an offering to nothingness,
A very little bit of precious wine . . .

Who willed your loss, O liquor?
Did I perhaps obey the soothsayer?
Perhaps the trouble of my heart,
Thinking of blood, pouring the wine?

After a pink vapor
The sea with equal purity recovered
Its customary transparency . . .

That wine lost, the waves intoxicated! . . .
I saw leaping in the bitter air
The most profound figures . . .

GUILLAUME APOLLINAIRE

Born in Rome, 1880; died in Paris, 1918

GUILLAUME (or Wilhelm) Albert Wladimir Alexandre Apollinaire (or Apollinaris) de Kostrowitzky was born in Rome, the illegitimate son of an Italian nobleman and a Polish girl of aristocratic background. He never saw his father after 1885. Kostrowitzky spent his school years in the South of France, arriving in Paris in 1899. After a brief Belgian idyll and a few odd jobs in Paris, he spent a year (1901-2) in the Rhineland as a tutor, vacationing in many parts of Germany and Austria-Hungary and assiduously courting his fellow employee, an English governess, whom he continued to pursue in London in 1903 and 1904, to no avail. Finally established in Paris, Kostrowitzky gradually acquired a solid reputation as a writer (using his last Christian name as a surname-de-plume) and as an art critic (he was a friend of the Cubist and Futurist painters), earning his living through journalistic assignments and by editing and sometimes composing erotica in prose and verse.

After the outbreak of war in 1914, Apollinaire, though not a native of France, enlisted, serving first in the artillery, then in the infantry as a second lieutenant. In March 1916 he was wounded in the temple by a shell fragment and underwent several operations. He was not discharged, but (in 1917) served for a time as a censor, then was given a sinecure in the colonial ministry. He married in May 1918. Two days before the Armistice he died of influenza.

Apollinaire's first volume of poetry (he had already published individual poems in magazines) was *Le Bestiaire ou Cortège d'Orphée* (1911), a series of witty and bittersweet jingles about animals, illustrated by Dufy. Probably his strongest collection, *Alcools*

(1913), contained the best poems he had written between 1898 and 1913: scenes and legends of the Rhine, poems of his fruitless love for the English governess (particularly the famous "Chanson du Mal-aimé"—Song of the Unloved Man); love poems for the artist Marie Laurencin, impressions of itinerant acrobats like those his friend Picasso painted, the poetical record of melancholy promenades in Paris ("Zone," "Le Pont Mirabeau"), visions of autumn and various imaginative pieces. The poems of *Alcools* are in a variety of forms, from rhymed and unrhymed free verse to stanzas like those of popular songs; their tone is now ironic, now moody, now dreamy. The absence of punctuation in this collection started a continuing trend. "Les Colchiques" (The Meadow-Saffrons, first published in the magazine *La Phalange* in November 1907), with its repetitions of words and of muted sounds, and with its subtly over-syllabled alexandrines, is a prime example of Apollinaire's art. In *La Phalange* the date of composition was given as 1902 and the place as the German villa where Apollinaire tutored, but some scholars find this impossible.

In 1917 the poet published a small book of six lovely pieces, *Vitam Impendere Amori* (To Spend Life on Love). *Calligrammes,* which appeared in 1918, contains poems written between 1913 and 1916. In this volume free verse becomes much more prevalent, while several poems are arranged typographically to form the object (automobile, dove) mentioned in their titles. The chief subjects are Apollinaire's experiences and impressions of war. Among the most famous pieces are "La petite Auto," on the 1914 mobilization, and the final poem, "La jolie Rousse" (The Pretty Redhead—Apollinaire's fiancée), on the tension between "order" and "adventure" in the poet's life and art.

Many sketches and confidential collections of poems were published posthumously: *Il y a* (There Is; 1925), *Poèmes à Lou* (1947 and 1955), *Le Guetteur mélancolique* (The Melancholy Watcher, 1952) and various others to be found in the 1956 edition of the complete poetic works.

Apollinaire also wrote some fine tales (especially those collected in the volume *L'Hérésiarque et Cie*—The Heresiarch and Co., 1910), plays (the most famous being *Les Mamelles de Tirésias*—Tiresias's Breasts, 1918), influential art criticism (particularly *Les Peintres cubistes*, 1913), prose sketches of Parisian life (*Le Flâneur des deux rives*—Stroller on Both Banks, 1918) and other prose items.

Les Colchiques

Le pré est vénéneux mais joli en automne
Les vaches y paissant
Lentement s'empoisonnent
Le colchique couleur de cerne et de lilas
Y fleurit tes yeux sont comme cette fleur-là
Violâtres comme leur cerne et comme cet automne
Et ma vie pour tes yeux lentement s'empoisonne

Les enfants de l'école viennent avec fracas
Vêtus de hoquetons et jouant de l'harmonica
Ils cueillent les colchiques qui sont comme des mères
Filles de leurs filles et sont couleur de tes paupières
Qui battent comme les fleurs battent au vent dément

Le gardien du troupeau chante tout doucement
Tandis que lentes et meuglant les vaches abandonnent
Pour toujours ce grand pré mal fleuri par l'automne

The Meadow-Saffrons

The meadow is poisonous but pretty in autumn
The cows grazing there
Are slowly poisoned
The meadow-saffron like bruised flesh and lilacs in color
Blooms there your eyes are like that flower
Purplish like their dark ring and like this autumn
And my life for your eyes is slowly poisoned

The schoolchildren come with a clatter
Dressed in smocks and playing the harmonica
They pick the saffrons which are like mothers
Daughters of their daughters and are the color of your eyelids
Which beat as the flowers beat in the crazy wind

The keeper of the herd sings very softly
While slowly and lowing the cows abandon
For ever this great meadow with its evil autumn flowers

JULES SUPERVIELLE

Born in Montevideo, 1884; died in Paris, 1960

UNATTACHED to any literary group or movement, but firmly loyal to humanity and the aspirations of the present age; creating his style slowly and, through constant revision and renewed self-examination, moving toward a unique personal expression and at the same time a fuller assimilation of the traditional values of French poetry, Supervielle acquired one of the purest lyrical voices of the twentieth century, discreet and magical. His pantheistic world is one of constant metamorphosis, of the transposition of familiar things to the sky, to the sea, in a troubling disorientation that illuminates their essence. Imaginative, sometimes whimsical visions of the creation of the world; perennial wonder in the presence of animals and trees; strange tableaux of the continued terrestrial existence of the dead; uneasy auscultations of the bodily organs (the poet was a victim of insomnia and heart trouble): these are some of the typical Superviellian preoccupations. The poet's hard-won fluency, delicacy and naturalness disguise his mastery of a great range of free and fixed forms.

Supervielle was born in Uruguay, where his family was in charge of a bank. His father (from Béarn) and his mother (from the Basque country) both died in France before he was a year old. Supervielle lived in South America with an uncle from 1886 to 1894, when he was sent to school in Paris. He settled in Paris, but made frequent trips to his native country all his life. It was in Uruguay that he was vacationing when the Second World War began and there that he spent the war years. In 1946 he returned to Paris as an honorary cultural attaché of Uruguay's embassy to France. From 1949 on, he was the recipient of several important literary awards.

The poet's earliest book of verse, *Brumes du passé* (Mists of the Past), was published when he was sixteen. The volume *Comme des voiliers* (Like Sailing Ships) appeared in 1910, *Poèmes* in 1919 and his first really important collection, *Débarcadères* (Landing Stages, impressions of the pampas and South American ports of call), in 1922. His finest volumes of poetry are *Gravitations* (1925, revised 1932); *Le Forçat innocent* (The Innocent Convict, 1930, containing the 1927 collection *Oloron-Sainte-Marie* and the 1928 sequence *Saisir*—To Grasp); *Les Amis inconnus* (The Unknown Friends, 1934); *La Fable du Monde* (The Fable of the World, 1938); and *1939–1945* (published 1946). The tone of this last-named volume, which includes the *Poèmes de la France malheureuse* (Poems of France's Misfortune, first published in Argentina and Switzerland in 1942), is one of quiet sadness and nostalgia, never of bitterness or vindictiveness. Other collections of poetry include *Oublieuse Mémoire* (Forgetful Memory, 1949), *Naissances* (Births, 1951), *L'Escalier* (The Staircase, 1956) and *Le Corps tragique* (The Tragic Body, 1959), which contains some translations from the Spanish poets Lorca and Guillén.

The two poems included here are "Réveil" (Awakening) from *Gravitations*, and "Dans la forêt sans heures" (In the hourless forest) from *Le Forçat innocent*.

Supervielle also wrote many short stories whose fantastic themes recall those of his best poems, especially the stories in the 1931 volume *L'Enfant de la haute mer* (The Child of the High Seas) and the 1938 *L'Arche de Noé* (Noah's Ark). He also wrote imaginative novels and plays.

Réveil

Le monde me quitte, ce tapis, ce livre,
Vous vous en allez;
Le balcon devient un nuage libre
Entre les volets.

Ah! chacun pour soi les quatre murs partent
Me tournant le dos
Et comme une barque au loin les commandent
D'invisibles flots.

Le plafond se plaint de son cœur de mouette
Qui se serre en lui,
Le parquet mirant une horreur secrète
A poussé un cri,
Comme si tombait un homme à la mer
D'un mât invisible
Et couronné d'air.

"Dans la forêt sans heures"

Dans la forêt sans heures
On abat un grand arbre.
Un vide vertical
Tremble en forme de fût
Près du tronc étendu.

Cherchez, cherchez oiseaux,
La place de vos nids
Dans ce haut souvenir
Tant qu'il murmure encore.

Awakening

The world is leaving me, this carpet, this book,
You are going away;
The balcony becomes a free cloud
Between the shutters.

Ah! the four walls depart, each on its own,
Turning their back on me,
And like a boat from afar they are controlled
By invisible waves.

The ceiling complains of its seagull's heart
Constricting within it;
The floor, reflecting a secret horror,
Has uttered a cry,
As if a man were falling into the sea
From an invisible mast
Crowned with air.

"In the hourless forest"

In the hourless forest
A tall tree is being felled.
A vertical void
Trembles in the form of a shaft
Near the outstretched trunk.

Search, birds, search,
For the site of your nests
In this high memory
While it is still murmuring.

SAINT-JOHN PERSE

Born on Saint-Léger-les-Feuilles, 1887;
died on Presqu'île-de-Giens, 1975

BORN on a Caribbean island (off Guadeloupe) which his family
of planters owned, Alexis Saint-Léger Léger was sent to
France for his education in 1898. In his student days he made the
acquaintance of several important poets. He was at the University
of Bordeaux when he wrote his first short collection, *Images à
Crusoé* (Pictures for Robinson Crusoe, 1909), nostalgic poems about
his West Indian childhood. The poet's first major volume (in-
corporating the Crusoe pieces) was *Éloges* (Praises, 1911; definitive
edition, including a few later poems, 1948), a majestic tribute to
his island home.

The diplomatic career of Saint-Léger Léger began in 1914. From
1916 to 1921 he was an embassy secretary in Peking. His impres-
sions of the East were transformed poetically in *Anabase* (Anabasis,
1924), the symbolic epic of a great empire-building journey
directed by Prince and Poet; *Anabase* was the first book published
under the pseudonym Saint-John Perse. Having greatly impressed
Aristide Briand during the course of the 1921 Washington Dis-
armament Conference, Saint-Léger Léger entered the Foreign
Ministry. He became Secretary-General of the French Foreign
Office in 1933.

Upon the establishment of the Vichy government in 1940,
Saint-Léger Léger was deprived of his post, and the manuscripts
of all his poetry since 1924 were destroyed. He left France for the
United States, where he lived in Washington, D.C. During the
Second World War he was Consultant on French Literature at
the Library of Congress. His closest friends in these war years
included T. S. Eliot, Archibald MacLeish and Francis Biddle.
This "exile" marked the triumph of the poet over the diplomat,

of Perse over Saint-Léger. The volume of wartime poems, *Exil* (definitive edition 1946), contains the famous sections "Pluies" (Rains) and "Neiges" (Snows).

The breath of deliverance, of new hope, of the poet's appreciation for his adoptive country, surges through the 1946 volume *Vents* (Winds). *Amers* (Seamarks, 1957) is a vast hymn to the sea and its meaning for the human spirit; the section "Étroits sont les vaisseaux" (Narrow are the vessels) is a compelling evocation of the amatory ritual. The volume *Chronique* (Chronicle; 1960) is the poet's assessment of his life in his advanced years; the part reproduced here is the final section of this work. *Oiseaux* (Birds, 1963) is a poem on the beauty of birds both in nature and in the art of Georges Braque. After the war, a series of literary awards,

Chronique

8

"... Grand âge, nous voici — et nos pas d'hommes vers l'issue. C'est assez d'engranger, il est temps d'éventer et d'honorer notre aire.

Demain, les grands orages maraudeurs, et l'éclair au travail ... Le caducée du ciel descend marquer la terre de son chiffre. L'alliance est fondée.

Ah! qu'une élite aussi se lève, de très grands arbres sur la terre, comme tribu de grandes âmes et qui nous tiennent en leur conseil ... Et la sévérité du soir descende, avec l'aveu de sa douceur, sur les chemins de pierre brûlante éclairés de lavande ...

Frémissement alors, à la plus haute tige engluée d'ambre, de la plus haute feuille mi-déliée sur son onglet d'ivoire.

Et nos actes s'éloignent dans leurs vergers d'éclairs ...

culminating in the Nobel Prize for 1960, brought Perse to the attention of a wider audience.

Like his fellow diplomat Claudel, Perse combines an intense lyrical gift with an epic scope and breadth, and both men exalt the sacred calling of the Poet. But Perse's outlook is completely secular; his major theme is the life of man in all eras and climes. The extraordinary range of his vocabulary, the wealth of prosodic resources within his free-verse lines and the seeming inexhaustibility of his bold imagery are firmly controlled by a sense of form and a symphonic interweaving of material that make each of his volumes one long poem and the totality of his work one consistent homage to man's universe.

Chronicle

8

"... *Great age, here we are—and our human steps toward the outcome. Enough of garnering; it is time to air and honor our threshing-floor.*

Tomorrow, the great raiding storms, and the lightning at work . . . The caduceus of heaven descends to brand the earth with its mark. The alliance is established.

Ah! may an elite also arise, very tall trees on the earth, like a tribe of great souls that will admit us to their council . . . And may the severity of evening descend, with the avowal of its gentleness, upon the roads of burning stone that are illumined by lavender . . .

A shudder then, to the highest stem sticky with amber, from the highest leaf half-unfurled on its ivory unguis.

And our acts move off into their orchards of lightning-flashes . . .

A d'autres d'édifier, parmi les schistes et les laves. A d'autres de lever les marbres à la ville.

Pour nous chante déjà plus hautaine aventure. Route frayée de main nouvelle, et feux portés de cime en cime...

Et ce ne sont point là chansons de toile pour gynécée, ni chansons de veillée, dites chansons de Reine de Hongrie, pour égrener le maïs rouge au fil rouillé des vieilles rapières de famille,

Mais chant plus grave, et d'autre glaive, comme chant d'honneur et de grand âge, et chant du Maître, seul au soir, à se frayer sa route devant l'âtre

— fierté de l'âme devant l'âme et fierté d'âme grandissante dans l'épée grande et bleue.

Et nos pensées déjà se lèvent dans la nuit comme les hommes de grande tente, avant le jour, qui marchent au ciel rouge portant leur selle sur l'épaule gauche.

Voici les lieux que nous laissons. Les fruits du sol sont sous nos murs, les eaux du ciel dans nos citernes, et les grandes meules de porphyre reposent sur le sable.

L'offrande, ô nuit, où la porter? et la louange, la fier?... Nous élevons à bout de bras, sur le plat de nos mains, comme couvée d'ailes naissantes, ce cœur enténébré de l'homme où fut l'avide, et fut l'ardent, et tant d'amour irrévélé...

Écoute, ô nuit, dans les préaux déserts et sous les arches solitaires, parmi les ruines saintes et l'émiettement des vieilles termitières, le grand pas souverain de l'âme sans tanière,

Comme aux dalles de bronze où rôderait un fauve.

*

Grand âge, nous voici. Prenez mesure du cœur d'homme."

Let others build, among the schists and the lavas. Let others bear the marbles to the city.

For us a loftier adventure is already singing. A trail blazed by new hands, and fires carried from summit to summit . . .

And these are not sewing songs for the gynaeceum nor songs for rural evenings, called songs of the Queen of Hungary, for shelling the red corn with the rusty edge of the old family rapiers,

But a more serious song, of another blade, like a song of honor and great age, and a song of the Master, alone in the evening, blazing his trail before the hearth

— pride of the soul before the soul and pride of a soul growing great in the great blue sword.

And already our thoughts rise up in the night like the dwellers in great tents, before daybreak, who walk beneath the red sky bearing their saddles on their left shoulders.

Here are the places we are leaving behind. The fruits of the soil are beneath our walls, the waters of the sky are in our cisterns, and the great porphyry millstones are resting on the sand.

The offering, O night, where shall we bring it? and the praise, where entrust it? . . . We raise up at arm's length, on the flat of our hands, like a brood of nascent wings, this benighted heart of man, where avidity was, and ardor, and so much unrevealed love . . .

Listen, O night, in the deserted courtyards and under the lonely bridge-arches, among the hallowed ruins and the crumbling of the old termites' nests, to the great sovereign tread of the lairless soul,

As if a wild beast were prowling on floors of bronze plate.

*

Great age, here we are. Take the measure of the heart of man."

PAUL ÉLUARD

Born in Saint-Denis, 1895; died at Charenton (Paris area), 1952

É LUARD, whose real name was Eugène Grindel, was born
not far from Paris. His family moved to the city in 1908;
Éluard's father was in charge of a small real estate office, where
the poet was employed for many years. Éluard, troubled by tuber-
culosis all his life, returned from two years in a Swiss sanatorium
in time to be drafted in 1914. After the war he joined the ranks of
the Dadaists, and with Breton and Aragon became one of the
founders of Surrealism. In 1924 he disappeared suddenly from
Paris and spent seven months traveling in the Far East and the
South Seas. His 1926 collection of love poetry, *Capitale de la douleur*
(Capital of Sorrow), made him the most respected of Surrealist
poets. Éluard's adhesion to the Communist party (and continuing
sympathy with its tenets after his exclusion in 1933) led to a break
with Breton and the Surrealist "orthodoxy." From 1939 until the
1940 Armistice, Éluard served actively in the army, then clandes-
tinely as one of the chief poets of the Resistance; he rejoined the
Communist party in 1942. After the war he made extensive trips
to Eastern Europe. He died in 1952.

Éluard is one of the greatest poets of love in French literature.
The glorification of woman and of the bonds between the sexes
was his lifelong major theme. His poems shifted between joy
and despair as a direct reflection of his personal experiences: his
marriage (1917) with Gala, beginning with great hopes, then
clouded and ending in divorce in 1930; his inspiring years with
Nusch until her unexpected death in 1946; new happiness and
optimism with Dominique in the last three years of his life.
Among his best volumes of love poems, in addition to *Capitale*,
are: *L'Amour la Poésie* (Love, Poetry; 1929); *La Vie immédiate* (Life

163

Seized Directly, 1932); *La Rose publique* (The Public Rose, 1934); *Les Yeux fertiles* (The Fertile Eyes, 1936); *Médieuses* (Mediatrices, 1938, later included in *Le Livre ouvert*—The Open Book, 1940, 1947), from which our first selection, "Au premier mot limpide," is taken; *Le Lit la Table* (The Bed, the Table; 1944); *Poésie ininterrompue* (Uninterrupted Poem, 1946); and *Le Phénix* (The Phoenix, 1951), the title poem of which is our second selection.

Whether using free verse, rhythmic prose, alexandrines of admirable purity and poise, or any of his other forms, Éluard again and again throughout his career achieved in modern times the warmth and the balance, the perfection of touch, that we admire in the finest French poets of the past. Only he among the Surrealist poets was able to range his free-floating images in patterns

Au premier mot limpide

Au premier mot limpide au premier rire de ta chair
La route épaisse disparaît
Tout recommence

La fleur timide la fleur sans air du ciel nocturne
Des mains voilées de maladresse
Des mains d'enfant

Des yeux levés vers ton visage et c'est le jour sur terre
La première jeunesse close
Le seul plaisir

Foyer de terre foyer d'odeurs et de rosée
Sans âge sans raisons sans liens
L'oubli sans ombre.

so meaningful and emotional despite their boldness and freshness.

Beginning in the thirties, more and more of Éluard's poems were of a political cast, poems directed against war, tyranny, poverty. Among these volumes are *Cours naturel* (Natural Course, 1938) and *Poèmes politiques* (1948). The poetry he wrote and distributed secretly during the Second World War was generally much simpler in style than his other work, being addressed to—and gratefully received by—a wider circle of readers. The chief volumes containing war poetry, besides *Le Livre ouvert*, are the 1942 book *Poésie et Vérité 1942* (Poetry and Truth 1942), which includes the famous hymn "Liberté," and *Au Rendez-vous allemand* (At the German Meeting Place; definitive edition 1946).

At the First Limpid Word

At the first limpid word at the first laughter of your flesh
The dense road disappears
Everything begins anew

The timid flower the airless flower of the night sky
Hands veiled in awkwardness
Child's hands

Eyes raised toward your face and it is day on earth
First-youth still in the bud
Pleasure alone

Hearth of earth hearth of fragrance and dew
Without age without reasons without bonds
Oblivion without shadow.

Le Phénix

Le Phénix, c'est le couple—Adam et
Eve—qui est et n'est pas le premier.

Je suis le dernier sur ta route
Le dernier printemps la dernière neige
Le dernier combat pour ne pas mourir

Et nous voici plus bas et plus haut que jamais.

★

Il y a de tout dans notre bûcher
Des pommes de pins des sarments
Mais aussi des fleurs plus fortes que l'eau

De la boue et de la rosée.

★

La flamme est sous nos pieds la flamme nous couronne
A nos pieds des insectes des oiseaux des hommes
Vont s'envoler

Ceux qui volent vont se poser.

★

Le ciel est clair la terre est sombre
Mais la fumée s'en va au ciel
Le ciel a perdu tous ses feux

La flamme est restée sur la terre.

★

La flamme est la nuée du cœur
Et toutes les branches du sang
Elle chante notre air

Elle dissipe la buée de notre hiver.

★

Nocturne et en horreur a flambé le chagrin
Les cendres ont fleuri en joie et en beauté
Nous tournons toujours le dos au couchant

Tout a la couleur de l'aurore.

The Phoenix

The Phoenix is the couple—Adam and
Eve—which is and is not the first.

I am the last on your path
The last springtime the last snow
The last struggle not to die

And here we are lower and higher than ever.

★

There is a little of everything in our pyre
Pine cones vine shoots
But also flowers stronger than water

Mud and dew.

★

The flame is beneath our feet the flame crowns us
At our feet insects birds men
Will fly away

Those who fly will alight.

★

The sky is bright the earth is dark
But the smoke goes up to the sky
The sky has lost all its fires

The flame has remained on earth.

★

The flame is the heart's cloud
And all the blood's branches
It sings our melody

It dispels the vapor of our winter.

★

In night and horror anguish blazed
The ashes have bloomed in joy and beauty
We still turn our back to the sunset

Everything has the color of dawn.

ARAGON

Born in Paris, 1897; died there, 1982

A RAGON'S Second World War poetry, which signaled a
departure in his subjects, style and outlook, if not in the
basic themes of his work, is the part of his extensive poetic *œuvre*
that has made the greatest mark so far, and it is appropriate to
represent the poet here by one of these inspiring pieces.

Louis Aragon was born in Paris, where his family ran a pension.
Like Breton, he was an army doctor during the First World War.
After that war he became one of the most brilliant members of
Dadaist and Surrealist circles. His prose book of Parisian impres-
sions, *Le Paysan de Paris* (The Peasant of Paris, 1926), is one of the
finest monuments of the "classical" period of Surrealism. His
earliest volumes of poetry, *Feu de joie* (Bonfire, 1920) and *Le
Mouvement perpétuel* (Perpetual Motion, 1926), were articulately
unpolitical. But two great events were in the offing. In 1927
Aragon joined the Communist party; though hesitant at first, he
has never swerved from this firm commitment, which led to his
break with Breton in 1932. And in 1928 he met the Russian-born
writer Elsa Triolet, who became his wife and the inspiration of
his literary production.

Between 1930 and 1936 Aragon made frequent trips to the Soviet
Union. The 1931 collection of poems, *Persécuté persécuteur* (Perse-
cuted Persecutor), opened with the inflammatory piece "Front
rouge" (Red Front), which upset the authorities. By 1934 and the
volume *Hourra l'Oural* (Hurrah Urals) Aragon's party line was
perfect but his poetic vein was dry. He published no more poetry
before World War II.

Aragon fought actively until the 1940 Armistice, then became
one of the leaders of the Resistance in word and deed. The shock

of the war, the defeat of his beloved country and the enforced separation from his wife contributed toward the creation of his most moving poetry. The first wartime volume (1941, definitive edition 1946) was *Le Crève-Cœur* (Heartbreak), from which our selection is taken. "Les Lilas et les roses," written in July 1940 and first published in the newspaper *Le Figaro* in September of that year, commemorates the retreat from the Battle of the North and the fall of Paris. Like many of the other war pieces, it uses simple language musically in classical meters (here alexandrines), pays homage to the physical beauty, the geography and the history of France (though all communism is international in orientation, Aragon's made him love his country more) and makes use of Christian images (even the form of the litany in this case), apparently in order to speak to the many. But unlike some of the pieces contemporary with it, "Les Lilas et les roses" is not marred by Aragon's specious innovations in rhyme. Among the other wartime volumes are *Le Musée Grévin* (1943) and *La Diane française* (The French Reveille, 1945).

Several volumes of poetry, closer in style to the war pieces than to anything that had preceded, appeared after the end of the conflict, including *Le Voyage de Hollande* (The Trip to Holland; 1964). The best of these books is probably the varied auto-biographical mélange *Le Roman inachevé* (The Uncompleted Novel, 1956). On the basis of these works one would not hesitate to classify Aragon as the greatest twentieth-century French popular poet, in the tradition of a Béranger or a Prévert, were it not for the highly intellectual elements in his writing and the verbal abandon remaining from his Surrealist days.

A fine prose stylist, Aragon also wrote several novels, of which the least political has been the most successful: *La Semaine sainte* (Holy Week; 1958). He was the director of the weekly newspaper *Les Lettres françaises*. In 1957 he won the Lenin Peace Prize.

Les Lilas et les roses

O mois des floraisons mois des métamorphoses
Mai qui fut sans nuage et Juin poignardé
Je n'oublierai jamais les lilas ni les roses
Ni ceux que le printemps dans ses plis a gardés

Je n'oublierai jamais l'illusion tragique
Le cortège des cris la foule et le soleil
Les chars chargés d'amour les dons de la Belgique
L'air qui tremble et la route à ce bourdon d'abeilles
Le triomphe imprudent qui prime la querelle
Le sang que préfigure en carmin le baiser
Et ceux qui vont mourir debout dans les tourelles
Entourés de lilas par un peuple grisé

Je n'oublierai jamais les jardins de la France
Semblables aux missels des siècles disparus
Ni le trouble des soirs l'énigme du silence
Les roses tout le long du chemin parcouru
Le démenti des fleurs au vent de la panique
Aux soldats qui passaient sur l'aile de la peur
Aux vélos délirants aux canons ironiques
Au pitoyable accoutrement des faux campeurs

Mais je ne sais pourquoi ce tourbillon d'images
Me ramène toujours au même point d'arrêt
A Sainte-Marthe Un général De noirs ramages
Une villa normande au bord de la forêt
Tout se tait L'ennemi dans l'ombre se repose
On nous a dit ce soir que Paris s'est rendu
Je n'oublierai jamais les lilas ni les roses
Et ni les deux amours que nous avons perdus

Bouquets du premier jour lilas lilas des Flandres
Douceur de l'ombre dont la mort farde les joues
Et vous bouquets de la retraite roses tendres
Couleur de l'incendie au loin roses d'Anjou

172

The Lilacs and the Roses

O months of flowerings months of metamorphoses
May that was cloudless and June that was stabbed
I shall never forget the lilacs or the roses
Or those whom the spring kept within its folds

I shall never forget the tragic illusion
The cortège of cries the crowd and the sun
The tanks burdened with love the gifts of Belgium
The trembling air and the road with that humming of bees
The thoughtless triumph that anticipates the conflict
The blood prefigured in carmine by the kiss
And those who are to die standing in the turrets
Encircled with lilacs by an intoxicated multitude

I shall never forget the gardens of France
Like the missals of vanished centuries
Or the agitation in the evenings the enigma of the silence
The roses all along the road that was traveled
The flowers that gave the lie to the wind of panic
To the soldiers passing by on the wing of fear
To the frenzied bicycles to the ironic cannons
To the pitiful get-up of the mock campers

But I do not know why this whirlwind of images
Always leads me back to the same stopping place
To Sainte-Marthe A general Black patterns of foliage
A Norman villa at the edge of the forest
Everything is still The enemy is resting in the shade
We were told this evening that Paris has surrendered
I shall never forget the lilacs or the roses
Or the two loves that we have lost

Bouquets of the first day lilacs lilacs of Flanders
Sweetness of the shade whose cheeks death rouges
And you bouquets of the retreat tender roses
Color of far-off fires roses of Anjou

YVES BONNEFOY

Born in Tours, 1923

AMONG the poets whose reputations have been established
since the Second World War, Yves Bonnefoy is outstanding.
He has identified his anguish and hesitant joys with the perennial
metaphysical problems of mankind, and has clothed them in a
personal language worthy of his greatest predecessors in French
poetry.

Bonnefoy was born in Tours, moving to Paris when he was
twenty. His studies were in philosophy and art history. After a
first brief book of Surrealist inspiration, *Traité du pianiste* (Treatise
of the Pianist, 1946), no longer in print, he observed a long silence.
Then in 1953 came his first major volume, *Du mouvement et de
l'immobilité de Douve* (On the Motion and Motionlessness of
Douve). In it the death of the loved one, Douve, brings first only
sorrow, but later the acceptance of death as an indispensable and
fructifying element of existence, and the eventual immortality of
Douve in the memory of the survivor (pivotal symbols of the
phoenix and the salamander). The 1958 volume *Hier régnant
désert* (When Yesterday Was Reigning as a Desert) moves from a
threat of apathy and near-despair toward the hope of dawn and
new beginnings. *Pierre écrite* (Inscribed Stone, 1959, definitive
edition 1965), renewing the art of the Hellenistic epitaph, mingles
the voices of the dead with the activities and memories of the
living during a summer and autumn in Southern France.

These three volumes, slender but slowly matured and retaining
nothing non-essential, cannot be described as "collections":
although the poems they contain can be read and enjoyed sepa-
rately, it is the movement within the volume and the carefully
worked out interplay of recurring words and images that reveal

the final meaning. The willed reduction of vocabulary, as well as the sensitive personal handling of traditional meters and poetic devices, makes Bonnefoy to a great extent a modern counterpart of Racine. Bonnefoy's great seriousness of purpose is evident. He objects to a poetry that merely mirrors the objects of the outside world. He sees poetry as an arena of incessant combat between form and essence, as a force to make men just, as an effort whose purpose is salvation.

The two poems presented here are from the final section, "A une Terre d'aube" (To a Land of Dawn), of *Hier régnant désert*. Both combine decasyllabic lines with alexandrines, rhyme with subtle assonance. Both use constructively and bring to fruition images introduced earlier in the book. "Ici, toujours ici" was first published in the *Mercure de France* in May 1958; "Aube, fille des larmes" was not pre-published separately.

Two shorter poem cycles make up the 1963 volume *Anti-Platon*, which recalls the mood and themes of *Douve* and is in part a

Ici, toujours ici

Ici, dans le lieu clair. Ce n'est plus l'aube,
C'est déjà la journée aux dicibles désirs.
Des mirages d'un chant dans ton rêve il ne reste
Que ce scintillement de pierres à venir.

Ici, et jusqu'au soir. La rose d'ombres
Tournera sur les murs. La rose d'heures
Défleurira sans bruit. Les dalles claires
Mèneront à leur gré ces pas épris du jour.

Ici, toujours ici. Pierres sur pierres
Ont bâti le pays dit par le souvenir.
A peine si le bruit de fruits simples qui tombent
Enfièvre encore en toi le temps qui va guérir.

rewarding expansion of material that dates back to the 1940's. Bonnefoy's prose essays on art and literature are collected in the volumes *L'Improbable* (1959) and *Un Rêve fait à Mantoue* (A Dream Experienced at Mantua, 1967), which includes the 1961 collection *La Seconde Simplicité*. The poet has also written a biography of Rimbaud (1961) and works of art history that include studies of French Gothic murals (1954), of the artist Miró (1967) and of artistic activity in Rome in the year 1630 (1967). He has also translated six Shakespeare plays; some of his versions have been performed in France.

Bonnefoy has traveled widely in Europe and North America for his art studies. He has given informal courses on modern French poetry at several universities in the United States. In France he divides his time between Paris and Provence, working on eagerly awaited new books.

Here, Always Here

Here, in the bright place. It is no longer dawn,
It is already day with its expressible desires.
Of the mirages of a song in your dream there remains
Only this sparkling of future stones.

Here, and until evening. The rose of shadows
Will turn on the walls. The rose of hours
Will lose its petals noiselessly. The bright flagstones
Will lead where they like these footsteps in love with day.

Here, always here. Stones on stones
Have built the country told by memory.
The noise of falling simple fruits just barely
Maintains in you the fever of the season which will heal.

"Aube, fille des larmes, rétablis"

Aube, fille des larmes, rétablis
La chambre dans sa paix de chose grise
Et le cœur dans son ordre. Tant de nuit
Demandait à ce feu qu'il décline et s'achève,
Il nous faut bien veiller près du visage mort.
A peine a-t-il changé ... Le navire des lampes
Entrera-t-il au port qu'il avait demandé,
Sur les tables d'ici la flamme faite cendre
Grandira-t-elle ailleurs dans une autre clarté?
Aube, soulève, prends le visage sans ombre,
Colore peu à peu le temps recommencé.

"Dawn, daughter of tears, reestablish"

Dawn, daughter of tears, reestablish
The room in its gray thing's peace
And the heart in its order. So much night
Demanded that that fire should abate and finish.
We must keep watch by the dead face.
It has barely changed . . . Will the ship of the lamps
Enter the port it had asked for,
Will the flame fallen to ash on the tables of this place
Wax elsewhere in another brightness?
Dawn, raise up, take the shadowless face,
Color little by little the time that is beginning again.

PICTURE SOURCES AND CREDITS

(BN stands for Bibliothèque Nationale, Paris.)

CHARLES D'ORLÉANS (p. 14). ABOVE: Scene of declaration of feudal homage to the Duke on an inventory document of a fief dated May 12, 1460 (from the decorated initial on folio 1 of document Q 1 477 1, Archives Nationales, Paris); *photo courtesy of Archives Nationales.* BELOW: Manuscript of the *rondeau* "Le temps a laissié son manteau" in the Duke's personal album of his poetry; the word "brouderie" (line 3) and the last five lines are in the poet's own hand (from folio 365 of MS fr. 25458, Département des Manuscrits, BN); *photo courtesy of BN.*

FRANÇOIS VILLON (p. 18). (No known portrait.) Page with opening of "L'Épitaphe" from the first dated edition of Villon's works, published by Pierre Levet in 1489 (Réserve des Imprimés, BN); *photo courtesy of BN.*

CLÉMENT MAROT (p. 24). (No portrait is now considered absolutely authentic.) The painting by Corneille de Lyon in the Louvre, reproduced here, is presumed to be a likeness of the poet; *photo courtesy of Service de Documentation Photographique de la Réunion des Musées Nationaux, Versailles.*

MAURICE SCÈVE (p. 28). Woodcut from the first edition of *Delie*, 1544 (Réserve des Imprimés, BN); *photo courtesy of BN.*

LOUISE LABÉ (p. 32). Engraving by H. Dubouchet after a portrait by Pierre (II) Woeriot, or Woeiriot (Cabinet des Estampes, BN); *photo courtesy of BN.*

JOACHIM DU BELLAY (p. 36). Pencil drawing by an artist of the school of Jean Cousin the Younger (Cabinet des Estampes, BN); *photo courtesy of BN.*

PIERRE DE RONSARD (p. 42). Engraving by Granthomme, about 1560 (Cabinet des Estampes, BN); *photo courtesy of BN.*

FRANÇOIS DE MALHERBE (p. 48). Engraving by Vorstermann after Dumoustier (Cabinet des Estampes, BN); *photo courtesy of BN.*

MARC-ANTOINE GÉRARD DE SAINT-AMANT (p. 54). (No portrait exists.) Title page of 1633 second edition of *Les Œuvres et Suitte des Œuvres* (Département des Imprimés, BN); *photo courtesy of BN.*

JEAN DE LA FONTAINE (p. 58). Painting by de Troy (Bibliothèque Publique, Geneva); the poet's name is on the original; *photo courtesy of Bibliothèque Publique, Geneva.*

FRANÇOIS-MARIE AROUET, DIT VOLTAIRE (p. 64). Painting by Nicolas de Largillière, 1718; this is the portrait mentioned on p. 67 (owned by M. Massimo Uleri, Paris, who has bequeathed it to the Musée de Versailles); *photo courtesy of M. Uleri.*

ANDRÉ CHÉNIER (p. 70). Painting by Suvée, 1794 (Cabinet des Estampes, BN); *photo courtesy of BN.*

ALPHONSE DE LAMARTINE (p. 76). Lithograph after A. Carrière, 1859 (Cabinet des Estampes, BN); *photo courtesy of BN.*

ALFRED DE VIGNY (p. 82). Lithograph after Devéria (Cabinet des Estampes, BN); *photo courtesy of BN.*

VICTOR HUGO (p. 88). Photograph from the early 1850's (Cabinet des Estampes, BN); *photo courtesy of BN.*

GÉRARD DE NERVAL (p. 94). Photograph by Nadar (Cabinet des Estampes, BN); *photo courtesy of BN.*

ALFRED DE MUSSET (p. 98). Engraving by Pollet after a painting by Landelle (Cabinet des Estampes, BN); *photo courtesy of BN.*

THÉOPHILE GAUTIER (p. 104). Photograph by J. Thierry (Cabinet des Estampes, BN); *photo courtesy of BN.*

CHARLES BAUDELAIRE (p. 110). Photograph by Nadar (Cabinet des Estampes, BN); *photo courtesy of BN.*

STÉPHANE MALLARMÉ (p. 116). Photograph (Cabinet des Estampes, BN); *photo courtesy of BN.*

PAUL VERLAINE (p. 120). Photograph (Cabinet des Estampes, BN); *photo courtesy of BN.*

ARTHUR RIMBAUD (p. 126). Photograph by Carjat (Cabinet des Estampes, BN); *photo courtesy of BN.*

PAUL CLAUDEL (p. 132). Photograph; *photo courtesy of French Cultural Services, N.Y.*

PAUL VALÉRY (p. 138). Photograph; *photo courtesy of French Cultural Services, N.Y.*

GUILLAUME APOLLINAIRE (p. 144). Photograph (in hospital, 1916); *photo courtesy of French Cultural Services, N.Y.*

JULES SUPERVIELLE (p. 150). Photograph, 1939, by Gisèle Freund.

SAINT-JOHN PERSE (p. 156). Photograph, 1951, by Hessler in Washington.

PAUL ÉLUARD (p. 162). Photograph; *photo courtesy of French Cultural Services, N.Y.*

ARAGON (p. 168). Photograph; *photo courtesy of French Cultural Services, N.Y.*

YVES BONNEFOY (p. 174). Photograph; *photo courtesy of Mercure de France, Paris.*

A CATALOG OF SELECTED
DOVER BOOKS
IN ALL FIELDS OF INTEREST

A CATALOG OF SELECTED DOVER
BOOKS IN ALL FIELDS OF INTEREST

CONCERNING THE SPIRITUAL IN ART, Wassily Kandinsky. Pioneering work by father of abstract art. Thoughts on color theory, nature of art. Analysis of earlier masters. 12 illustrations. 80pp. of text. 5⅜ x 8½. 0-486-23411-8

CELTIC ART: The Methods of Construction, George Bain. Simple geometric techniques for making Celtic interlacements, spirals, Kells-type initials, animals, humans, etc. Over 500 illustrations. 160pp. 9 x 12. (Available in U.S. only.) 0-486-22923-8

AN ATLAS OF ANATOMY FOR ARTISTS, Fritz Schider. Most thorough reference work on art anatomy in the world. Hundreds of illustrations, including selections from works by Vesalius, Leonardo, Goya, Ingres, Michelangelo, others. 593 illustrations. 192pp. 7⅛ x 10¼. 0-486-20241-0

CELTIC HAND STROKE-BY-STROKE (Irish Half-Uncial from "The Book of Kells"): An Arthur Baker Calligraphy Manual, Arthur Baker. Complete guide to creating each letter of the alphabet in distinctive Celtic manner. Covers hand position, strokes, pens, inks, paper, more. Illustrated. 48pp. 8¼ x 11. 0-486-24336-2

EASY ORIGAMI, John Montroll. Charming collection of 32 projects (hat, cup, pelican, piano, swan, many more) specially designed for the novice origami hobbyist. Clearly illustrated easy-to-follow instructions insure that even beginning papercrafters will achieve successful results. 48pp. 8¼ x 11. 0-486-27298-2

BLOOMINGDALE'S ILLUSTRATED 1886 CATALOG: Fashions, Dry Goods and Housewares, Bloomingdale Brothers. Famed merchants' extremely rare catalog depicting about 1,700 products: clothing, housewares, firearms, dry goods, jewelry, more. Invaluable for dating, identifying vintage items. Also, copyright-free graphics for artists, designers. Co-published with Henry Ford Museum & Greenfield Village. 160pp. 8¼ x 11. 0-486-25780-0

THE ART OF WORLDLY WISDOM, Baltasar Gracian. "Think with the few and speak with the many," "Friends are a second existence," and "Be able to forget" are among this 1637 volume's 300 pithy maxims. A perfect source of mental and spiritual refreshment, it can be opened at random and appreciated either in brief or at length. 128pp. 5⅜ x 8½. 0-486-44034-6

JOHNSON'S DICTIONARY: A Modern Selection, Samuel Johnson (E. L. McAdam and George Milne, eds.). This modern version reduces the original 1755 edition's 2,300 pages of definitions and literary examples to a more manageable length, retaining the verbal pleasure and historical curiosity of the original. 480pp. 5⅜₆ x 8¼. 0-486-44089-3

ADVENTURES OF HUCKLEBERRY FINN, Mark Twain, Illustrated by E. W. Kemble. A work of eternal richness and complexity, a source of ongoing critical debate, and a literary landmark, Twain's 1885 masterpiece about a barefoot boy's journey of self-discovery has enthralled readers around the world. This handsome clothbound reproduction of the first edition features all 174 of the original black-and-white illustrations. 368pp. 5⅜ x 8½. 0-486-44322-1

STICKLEY CRAFTSMAN FURNITURE CATALOGS, Gustav Stickley and L. & J. G. Stickley. Beautiful, functional furniture in two authentic catalogs from 1910. 594 illustrations, including 277 photos, show settles, rockers, armchairs, reclining chairs, bookcases, desks, tables. 183pp. 6½ x 9¼. 0-486-23838-5

AMERICAN LOCOMOTIVES IN HISTORIC PHOTOGRAPHS: 1858 to 1949, Ron Ziel (ed.). A rare collection of 126 meticulously detailed official photographs, called "builder portraits," of American locomotives that majestically chronicle the rise of steam locomotive power in America. Introduction. Detailed captions. xi+ 129pp. 9 x 12. 0-486-27393-8

AMERICA'S LIGHTHOUSES: An Illustrated History, Francis Ross Holland, Jr. Delightfully written, profusely illustrated fact-filled survey of over 200 American lighthouses since 1716. History, anecdotes, technological advances, more. 240pp. 8 x 10¾. 0-486-25576-X

TOWARDS A NEW ARCHITECTURE, Le Corbusier. Pioneering manifesto by founder of "International School." Technical and aesthetic theories, views of industry, economics, relation of form to function, "mass-production split" and much more. Profusely illustrated. 320pp. 6⅛ x 9¼. (Available in U.S. only.) 0-486-25023-7

HOW THE OTHER HALF LIVES, Jacob Riis. Famous journalistic record, exposing poverty and degradation of New York slums around 1900, by major social reformer. 100 striking and influential photographs. 233pp. 10 x 7⅞. 0-486-22012-5

FRUIT KEY AND TWIG KEY TO TREES AND SHRUBS, William M. Harlow. One of the handiest and most widely used identification aids. Fruit key covers 120 deciduous and evergreen species; twig key 160 deciduous species. Easily used. Over 300 photographs. 126pp. 5⅜ x 8½. 0-486-20511-8

COMMON BIRD SONGS, Dr. Donald J. Borror. Songs of 60 most common U.S. birds: robins, sparrows, cardinals, bluejays, finches, more–arranged in order of increasing complexity. Up to 9 variations of songs of each species. Cassette and manual 0-486-99911-4

ORCHIDS AS HOUSE PLANTS, Rebecca Tyson Northen. Grow cattleyas and many other kinds of orchids–in a window, in a case, or under artificial light. 63 illustrations. 148pp. 5⅜ x 8½. 0-486-23261-1

MONSTER MAZES, Dave Phillips. Masterful mazes at four levels of difficulty. Avoid deadly perils and evil creatures to find magical treasures. Solutions for all 32 exciting illustrated puzzles. 48pp. 8¼ x 11. 0-486-26005-4

MOZART'S DON GIOVANNI (DOVER OPERA LIBRETTO SERIES), Wolfgang Amadeus Mozart. Introduced and translated by Ellen H. Bleiler. Standard Italian libretto, with complete English translation. Convenient and thoroughly portable–an ideal companion for reading along with a recording or the performance itself. Introduction. List of characters. Plot summary. 121pp. 5¼ x 8½. 0-486-24944-1

FRANK LLOYD WRIGHT'S DANA HOUSE, Donald Hoffmann. Pictorial essay of residential masterpiece with over 160 interior and exterior photos, plans, elevations, sketches and studies. 128pp. 9¼ x 10¾. 0-486-29120-0

THE CLARINET AND CLARINET PLAYING, David Pino. Lively, comprehensive work features suggestions about technique, musicianship, and musical interpretation, as well as guidelines for teaching, making your own reeds, and preparing for public performance. Includes an intriguing look at clarinet history. "A godsend," *The Clarinet,* Journal of the International Clarinet Society. Appendixes. 7 illus. 320pp. 5⅜ x 8½. 0-486-40270-3

HOLLYWOOD GLAMOR PORTRAITS, John Kobal (ed.). 145 photos from 1926-49. Harlow, Gable, Bogart, Bacall; 94 stars in all. Full background on photographers, technical aspects. 160pp. 8⅜ x 11¼. 0-486-23352-9

THE RAVEN AND OTHER FAVORITE POEMS, Edgar Allan Poe. Over 40 of the author's most memorable poems: "The Bells," "Ulalume," "Israfel," "To Helen," "The Conqueror Worm," "Eldorado," "Annabel Lee," many more. Alphabetic lists of titles and first lines. 64pp. 5$\frac{3}{16}$ x 8¼. 0-486-26685-0

PERSONAL MEMOIRS OF U. S. GRANT, Ulysses Simpson Grant. Intelligent, deeply moving firsthand account of Civil War campaigns, considered by many the finest military memoirs ever written. Includes letters, historic photographs, maps and more. 528pp. 6⅛ x 9¼. 0-486-28587-1

ANCIENT EGYPTIAN MATERIALS AND INDUSTRIES, A. Lucas and J. Harris. Fascinating, comprehensive, thoroughly documented text describes this ancient civilization's vast resources and the processes that incorporated them in daily life, including the use of animal products, building materials, cosmetics, perfumes and incense, fibers, glazed ware, glass and its manufacture, materials used in the mummification process, and much more. 544pp. 6⅛ x 9¼. (Available in U.S. only.) 0-486-40446-3

RUSSIAN STORIES/RUSSKIE RASSKAZY: A Dual-Language Book, edited by Gleb Struve. Twelve tales by such masters as Chekhov, Tolstoy, Dostoevsky, Pushkin, others. Excellent word-for-word English translations on facing pages, plus teaching and study aids, Russian/English vocabulary, biographical/critical introductions, more. 416pp. 5⅜ x 8½. 0-486-26244-8

PHILADELPHIA THEN AND NOW: 60 Sites Photographed in the Past and Present, Kenneth Finkel and Susan Oyama. Rare photographs of City Hall, Logan Square, Independence Hall, Betsy Ross House, other landmarks juxtaposed with contemporary views. Captures changing face of historic city. Introduction. Captions. 128pp. 8¼ x 11. 0-486-25790-8

NORTH AMERICAN INDIAN LIFE: Customs and Traditions of 23 Tribes, Elsie Clews Parsons (ed.). 27 fictionalized essays by noted anthropologists examine religion, customs, government, additional facets of life among the Winnebago, Crow, Zuni, Eskimo, other tribes. 480pp. 6⅛ x 9¼. 0-486-27377-6

TECHNICAL MANUAL AND DICTIONARY OF CLASSICAL BALLET, Gail Grant. Defines, explains, comments on steps, movements, poses and concepts. 15-page pictorial section. Basic book for student, viewer. 127pp. 5⅜ x 8½. 0-486-21843-0

THE MALE AND FEMALE FIGURE IN MOTION: 60 Classic Photographic Sequences, Eadweard Muybridge. 60 true-action photographs of men and women walking, running, climbing, bending, turning, etc., reproduced from rare 19th-century masterpiece. vi + 121pp. 9 x 12. 0-486-24745-7

ANIMALS: 1,419 Copyright-Free Illustrations of Mammals, Birds, Fish, Insects, etc., Jim Harter (ed.). Clear wood engravings present, in extremely lifelike poses, over 1,000 species of animals. One of the most extensive pictorial sourcebooks of its kind. Captions. Index. 284pp. 9 x 12. 0-486-23766-4

1001 QUESTIONS ANSWERED ABOUT THE SEASHORE, N. J. Berrill and Jacquelyn Berrill. Queries answered about dolphins, sea snails, sponges, starfish, fishes, shore birds, many others. Covers appearance, breeding, growth, feeding, much more. 305pp. 5¼ x 8¼. 0-486-23366-9

ATTRACTING BIRDS TO YOUR YARD, William J. Weber. Easy-to-follow guide offers advice on how to attract the greatest diversity of birds: birdhouses, feeders, water and waterers, much more. 96pp. 5³⁄₁₆ x 8¼. 0-486-28927-3

MEDICINAL AND OTHER USES OF NORTH AMERICAN PLANTS: A Historical Survey with Special Reference to the Eastern Indian Tribes, Charlotte Erichsen-Brown. Chronological historical citations document 500 years of usage of plants, trees, shrubs native to eastern Canada, northeastern U.S. Also complete identifying information. 343 illustrations. 544pp. 6½ x 9¼. 0-486-25951-X

STORYBOOK MAZES, Dave Phillips. 23 stories and mazes on two-page spreads: Wizard of Oz, Treasure Island, Robin Hood, etc. Solutions. 64pp. 8¼ x 11. 0-486-23628-5

AMERICAN NEGRO SONGS: 230 Folk Songs and Spirituals, Religious and Secular, John W. Work. This authoritative study traces the African influences of songs sung and played by black Americans at work, in church, and as entertainment. The author discusses the lyric significance of such songs as "Swing Low, Sweet Chariot," "John Henry," and others and offers the words and music for 230 songs. Bibliography. Index of Song Titles. 272pp. 6½ x 9¼. 0-486-40271-1

MOVIE-STAR PORTRAITS OF THE FORTIES, John Kobal (ed.). 163 glamor, studio photos of 106 stars of the 1940s: Rita Hayworth, Ava Gardner, Marlon Brando, Clark Gable, many more. 176pp. 8⅜ x 11¼. 0-486-23546-7

YEKL and THE IMPORTED BRIDEGROOM AND OTHER STORIES OF YIDDISH NEW YORK, Abraham Cahan. Film Hester Street based on *Yekl* (1896). Novel, other stories among first about Jewish immigrants on N.Y.'s East Side. 240pp. 5⅜ x 8½. 0-486-22427-9

SELECTED POEMS, Walt Whitman. Generous sampling from *Leaves of Grass*. Twenty-four poems include "I Hear America Singing," "Song of the Open Road," "I Sing the Body Electric," "When Lilacs Last in the Dooryard Bloom'd," "O Captain! My Captain!"–all reprinted from an authoritative edition. Lists of titles and first lines. 128pp. 5³⁄₁₆ x 8¼. 0-486-26878-0

SONGS OF EXPERIENCE: Facsimile Reproduction with 26 Plates in Full Color, William Blake. 26 full-color plates from a rare 1826 edition. Includes "The Tyger," "London," "Holy Thursday," and other poems. Printed text of poems. 48pp. 5¼ x 7. 0-486-24636-1

THE BEST TALES OF HOFFMANN, E. T. A. Hoffmann. 10 of Hoffmann's most important stories: "Nutcracker and the King of Mice," "The Golden Flowerpot," etc. 458pp. 5⅜ x 8½. 0-486-21793-0

THE BOOK OF TEA, Kakuzo Okakura. Minor classic of the Orient: entertaining, charming explanation, interpretation of traditional Japanese culture in terms of tea ceremony. 94pp. 5⅜ x 8½. 0-486-20070-1

FRENCH STORIES/CONTES FRANÇAIS: A Dual-Language Book, Wallace Fowlie. Ten stories by French masters, Voltaire to Camus: "Micromegas" by Voltaire; "The Atheist's Mass" by Balzac; "Minuet" by de Maupassant; "The Guest" by Camus, six more. Excellent English translations on facing pages. Also French-English vocabulary list, exercises, more. 352pp. 5⅜ x 8½. 0-486-26443-2

CHICAGO AT THE TURN OF THE CENTURY IN PHOTOGRAPHS: 122 Historic Views from the Collections of the Chicago Historical Society, Larry A. Viskochil. Rare large-format prints offer detailed views of City Hall, State Street, the Loop, Hull House, Union Station, many other landmarks, circa 1904-1913. Introduction. Captions. Maps. 144pp. 9⅜ x 12¼. 0-486-24656-6

OLD BROOKLYN IN EARLY PHOTOGRAPHS, 1865-1929, William Lee Younger. Luna Park, Gravesend race track, construction of Grand Army Plaza, moving of Hotel Brighton, etc. 157 previously unpublished photographs. 165pp. 8⅞ x 11¾. 0-486-23587-4

THE MYTHS OF THE NORTH AMERICAN INDIANS, Lewis Spence. Rich anthology of the myths and legends of the Algonquins, Iroquois, Pawnees and Sioux, prefaced by an extensive historical and ethnological commentary. 36 illustrations. 480pp. 5⅜ x 8½. 0-486-25967-6

AN ENCYCLOPEDIA OF BATTLES: Accounts of Over 1,560 Battles from 1479 B.C. to the Present, David Eggenberger. Essential details of every major battle in recorded history from the first battle of Megiddo in 1479 B.C. to Grenada in 1984. List of Battle Maps. New Appendix covering the years 1967-1984. Index. 99 illustrations. 544pp. 6½ x 9¼. 0-486-24913-1

SAILING ALONE AROUND THE WORLD, Captain Joshua Slocum. First man to sail around the world, alone, in small boat. One of great feats of seamanship told in delightful manner. 67 illustrations. 294pp. 5⅜ x 8½. 0-486-20326-3

ANARCHISM AND OTHER ESSAYS, Emma Goldman. Powerful, penetrating, prophetic essays on direct action, role of minorities, prison reform, puritan hypocrisy, violence, etc. 271pp. 5⅜ x 8½. 0-486-22484-8

MYTHS OF THE HINDUS AND BUDDHISTS, Ananda K. Coomaraswamy and Sister Nivedita. Great stories of the epics; deeds of Krishna, Shiva, taken from puranas, Vedas, folk tales; etc. 32 illustrations. 400pp. 5⅜ x 8½. 0-486-21759-0

MY BONDAGE AND MY FREEDOM, Frederick Douglass. Born a slave, Douglass became outspoken force in antislavery movement. The best of Douglass' autobiographies. Graphic description of slave life. 464pp. 5⅜ x 8½. 0-486-22457-0

FOLLOWING THE EQUATOR: A Journey Around the World, Mark Twain. Fascinating humorous account of 1897 voyage to Hawaii, Australia, India, New Zealand, etc. Ironic, bemused reports on peoples, customs, climate, flora and fauna, politics, much more. 197 illustrations. 720pp. 5⅜ x 8½. 0-486-26113-1

THE PEOPLE CALLED SHAKERS, Edward D. Andrews. Definitive study of Shakers: origins, beliefs, practices, dances, social organization, furniture and crafts, etc. 33 illustrations. 351pp. 5⅜ x 8½. 0-486-21081-2

THE MYTHS OF GREECE AND ROME, H. A. Guerber. A classic of mythology, generously illustrated, long prized for its simple, graphic, accurate retelling of the principal myths of Greece and Rome, and for its commentary on their origins and significance. With 64 illustrations by Michelangelo, Raphael, Titian, Rubens, Canova, Bernini and others. 480pp. 5⅜ x 8½. 0-486-27584-1

PSYCHOLOGY OF MUSIC, Carl E. Seashore. Classic work discusses music as a medium from psychological viewpoint. Clear treatment of physical acoustics, auditory apparatus, sound perception, development of musical skills, nature of musical feeling, host of other topics. 88 figures. 408pp. 5⅜ x 8½. 0-486-21851-1

LIFE IN ANCIENT EGYPT, Adolf Erman. Fullest, most thorough, detailed older account with much not in more recent books, domestic life, religion, magic, medicine, commerce, much more. Many illustrations reproduce tomb paintings, carvings, hieroglyphs, etc. 597pp. 5⅜ x 8½. 0-486-22632-8

SUNDIALS, Their Theory and Construction, Albert Waugh. Far and away the best, most thorough coverage of ideas, mathematics concerned, types, construction, adjusting anywhere. Simple, nontechnical treatment allows even children to build several of these dials. Over 100 illustrations. 230pp. 5⅜ x 8½. 0-486-22947-5

THEORETICAL HYDRODYNAMICS, L. M. Milne-Thomson. Classic exposition of the mathematical theory of fluid motion, applicable to both hydrodynamics and aerodynamics. Over 600 exercises. 768pp. 6⅛ x 9¼. 0-486-68970-0

OLD-TIME VIGNETTES IN FULL COLOR, Carol Belanger Grafton (ed.). Over 390 charming, often sentimental illustrations, selected from archives of Victorian graphics—pretty women posing, children playing, food, flowers, kittens and puppies, smiling cherubs, birds and butterflies, much more. All copyright-free. 48pp. 9¼ x 12¼. 0-486-27269-9

PERSPECTIVE FOR ARTISTS, Rex Vicat Cole. Depth, perspective of sky and sea, shadows, much more, not usually covered. 391 diagrams, 81 reproductions of drawings and paintings. 279pp. 5⅜ x 8½. 0-486-22487-2

DRAWING THE LIVING FIGURE, Joseph Sheppard. Innovative approach to artistic anatomy focuses on specifics of surface anatomy, rather than muscles and bones. Over 170 drawings of live models in front, back and side views, and in widely varying poses. Accompanying diagrams. 177 illustrations. Introduction. Index. 144pp. 8⅜ x11¼. 0-486-26723-7

GOTHIC AND OLD ENGLISH ALPHABETS: 100 Complete Fonts, Dan X. Solo. Add power, elegance to posters, signs, other graphics with 100 stunning copyright-free alphabets: Blackstone, Dolbey, Germania, 97 more—including many lower-case, numerals, punctuation marks. 104pp. 8⅛ x 11. 0-486-24695-7

THE BOOK OF WOOD CARVING, Charles Marshall Sayers. Finest book for beginners discusses fundamentals and offers 34 designs. "Absolutely first rate . . . well thought out and well executed."—E. J. Tangerman. 118pp. 7¾ x 10⅝. 0-486-23654-4

ILLUSTRATED CATALOG OF CIVIL WAR MILITARY GOODS: Union Army Weapons, Insignia, Uniform Accessories, and Other Equipment, Schuyler, Hartley, and Graham. Rare, profusely illustrated 1846 catalog includes Union Army uniform and dress regulations, arms and ammunition, coats, insignia, flags, swords, rifles, etc. 226 illustrations. 160pp. 9 x 12. 0-486-24939-5

WOMEN'S FASHIONS OF THE EARLY 1900s: An Unabridged Republication of "New York Fashions, 1909," National Cloak & Suit Co. Rare catalog of mail-order fashions documents women's and children's clothing styles shortly after the turn of the century. Captions offer full descriptions, prices. Invaluable resource for fashion, costume historians. Approximately 725 illustrations. 128pp. 8⅜ x 11¼.

0-486-27276-1

HOW TO DO BEADWORK, Mary White. Fundamental book on craft from simple projects to five-bead chains and woven works. 106 illustrations. 142pp. 5⅜ x 8.

0-486-20697-1

THE 1912 AND 1915 GUSTAV STICKLEY FURNITURE CATALOGS, Gustav Stickley. With over 200 detailed illustrations and descriptions, these two catalogs are essential reading and reference materials and identification guides for Stickley furniture. Captions cite materials, dimensions and prices. 112pp. 6½ x 9¼. 0-486-26676-1

EARLY AMERICAN LOCOMOTIVES, John H. White, Jr. Finest locomotive engravings from early 19th century: historical (1804–74), main-line (after 1870), special, foreign, etc. 147 plates. 142pp. 11⅜ x 8¼. 0-486-22772-3

LITTLE BOOK OF EARLY AMERICAN CRAFTS AND TRADES, Peter Stockham (ed.). 1807 children's book explains crafts and trades: baker, hatter, cooper, potter, and many others. 23 copperplate illustrations. 140pp. 4⅝ x 6.

0-486-23336-7

VICTORIAN FASHIONS AND COSTUMES FROM HARPER'S BAZAR, 1867–1898, Stella Blum (ed.). Day costumes, evening wear, sports clothes, shoes, hats, other accessories in over 1,000 detailed engravings. 320pp. 9⅜ x 12¼.

0-486-22990-4

THE LONG ISLAND RAIL ROAD IN EARLY PHOTOGRAPHS, Ron Ziel. Over 220 rare photos, informative text document origin (1844) and development of rail service on Long Island. Vintage views of early trains, locomotives, stations, passengers, crews, much more. Captions. 8⅞ x 11¾. 0-486-26301-0

VOYAGE OF THE LIBERDADE, Joshua Slocum. Great 19th-century mariner's thrilling, first-hand account of the wreck of his ship off South America, the 35-foot boat he built from the wreckage, and its remarkable voyage home. 128pp. 5⅜ x 8½.

0-486-40022-0

TEN BOOKS ON ARCHITECTURE, Vitruvius. The most important book ever written on architecture. Early Roman aesthetics, technology, classical orders, site selection, all other aspects. Morgan translation. 331pp. 5⅜ x 8½. 0-486-20645-9

THE HUMAN FIGURE IN MOTION, Eadweard Muybridge. More than 4,500 stopped-action photos, in action series, showing undraped men, women, children jumping, lying down, throwing, sitting, wrestling, carrying, etc. 390pp. 7⅞ x 10⅝.

0-486-20204-6 Clothbd.

TREES OF THE EASTERN AND CENTRAL UNITED STATES AND CANADA, William M. Harlow. Best one-volume guide to 140 trees. Full descriptions, woodlore, range, etc. Over 600 illustrations. Handy size. 288pp. 4½ x 6⅜. 0-486-20395-6

GROWING AND USING HERBS AND SPICES, Milo Miloradovich. Versatile handbook provides all the information needed for cultivation and use of all the herbs and spices available in North America. 4 illustrations. Index. Glossary. 236pp. 5⅜ x 8½.

0-486-25058-X

BIG BOOK OF MAZES AND LABYRINTHS, Walter Shepherd. 50 mazes and labyrinths in all—classical, solid, ripple, and more—in one great volume. Perfect inexpensive puzzler for clever youngsters. Full solutions. 112pp. 8⅛ x 11. 0-486-22951-3

PIANO TUNING, J. Cree Fischer. Clearest, best book for beginner, amateur. Simple repairs, raising dropped notes, tuning by easy method of flattened fifths. No previous skills needed. 4 illustrations. 201pp. 5⅜ x 8½. 0-486-23267-0

HINTS TO SINGERS, Lillian Nordica. Selecting the right teacher, developing confidence, overcoming stage fright, and many other important skills receive thoughtful discussion in this indispensible guide, written by a world-famous diva of four decades' experience. 96pp. 5⅜ x 8½. 0-486-40094-8

THE COMPLETE NONSENSE OF EDWARD LEAR, Edward Lear. All nonsense limericks, zany alphabets, Owl and Pussycat, songs, nonsense botany, etc., illustrated by Lear. Total of 320pp. 5⅜ x 8½. (Available in U.S. only.) 0-486-20167-8

VICTORIAN PARLOUR POETRY: An Annotated Anthology, Michael R. Turner. 117 gems by Longfellow, Tennyson, Browning, many lesser-known poets. "The Village Blacksmith," "Curfew Must Not Ring Tonight," "Only a Baby Small," dozens more, often difficult to find elsewhere. Index of poets, titles, first lines. xxiii + 325pp. 5⅝ x 8¼. 0-486-27044-0

DUBLINERS, James Joyce. Fifteen stories offer vivid, tightly focused observations of the lives of Dublin's poorer classes. At least one, "The Dead," is considered a masterpiece. Reprinted complete and unabridged from standard edition. 160pp. $5\frac{3}{16}$ x 8¼. 0-486-26870-5

GREAT WEIRD TALES: 14 Stories by Lovecraft, Blackwood, Machen and Others, S. T. Joshi (ed.). 14 spellbinding tales, including "The Sin Eater," by Fiona McLeod, "The Eye Above the Mantel," by Frank Belknap Long, as well as renowned works by R. H. Barlow, Lord Dunsany, Arthur Machen, W. C. Morrow and eight other masters of the genre. 256pp. 5⅜ x 8½. (Available in U.S. only.) 0-486-40436-6

THE BOOK OF THE SACRED MAGIC OF ABRAMELIN THE MAGE, translated by S. MacGregor Mathers. Medieval manuscript of ceremonial magic. Basic document in Aleister Crowley, Golden Dawn groups. 268pp. 5⅜ x 8½. 0-486-23211-5

THE BATTLES THAT CHANGED HISTORY, Fletcher Pratt. Eminent historian profiles 16 crucial conflicts, ancient to modern, that changed the course of civilization. 352pp. 5⅜ x 8½. 0-486-41129-X

NEW RUSSIAN-ENGLISH AND ENGLISH-RUSSIAN DICTIONARY, M. A. O'Brien. This is a remarkably handy Russian dictionary, containing a surprising amount of information, including over 70,000 entries. 366pp. 4½ x 6⅛. 0-486-20208-9

NEW YORK IN THE FORTIES, Andreas Feininger. 162 brilliant photographs by the well-known photographer, formerly with *Life* magazine. Commuters, shoppers, Times Square at night, much else from city at its peak. Captions by John von Hartz. 181pp. 9¼ x 10¾. 0-486-23585-8

INDIAN SIGN LANGUAGE, William Tomkins. Over 525 signs developed by Sioux and other tribes. Written instructions and diagrams. Also 290 pictographs. 111pp. 6⅛ x 9¼. 0-486-22029-X

ANATOMY: A Complete Guide for Artists, Joseph Sheppard. A master of figure drawing shows artists how to render human anatomy convincingly. Over 460 illustrations. 224pp. 8⅜ x 11¼. 0-486-27279-6

MEDIEVAL CALLIGRAPHY: Its History and Technique, Marc Drogin. Spirited history, comprehensive instruction manual covers 13 styles (ca. 4th century through 15th). Excellent photographs; directions for duplicating medieval techniques with modern tools. 224pp. 8⅜ x 11¼. 0-486-26142-5

DRIED FLOWERS: How to Prepare Them, Sarah Whitlock and Martha Rankin. Complete instructions on how to use silica gel, meal and borax, perlite aggregate, sand and borax, glycerine and water to create attractive permanent flower arrangements. 12 illustrations. 32pp. 5⅜ x 8½. 0-486-21802-3

EASY-TO-MAKE BIRD FEEDERS FOR WOODWORKERS, Scott D. Campbell. Detailed, simple-to-use guide for designing, constructing, caring for and using feeders. Text, illustrations for 12 classic and contemporary designs. 96pp. 5⅜ x 8½. 0-486-25847-5

THE COMPLETE BOOK OF BIRDHOUSE CONSTRUCTION FOR WOODWORKERS, Scott D. Campbell. Detailed instructions, illustrations, tables. Also data on bird habitat and instinct patterns. Bibliography. 3 tables. 63 illustrations in 15 figures. 48pp. 5¼ x 8½. 0-486-24407-5

SCOTTISH WONDER TALES FROM MYTH AND LEGEND, Donald A. Mackenzie. 16 lively tales tell of giants rumbling down mountainsides, of a magic wand that turns stone pillars into warriors, of gods and goddesses, evil hags, powerful forces and more. 240pp. 5⅜ x 8½. 0-486-29677-6

THE HISTORY OF UNDERCLOTHES, C. Willett Cunnington and Phyllis Cunnington. Fascinating, well-documented survey covering six centuries of English undergarments, enhanced with over 100 illustrations: 12th-century laced-up bodice, footed long drawers (1795), 19th-century bustles, 19th-century corsets for men, Victorian "bust improvers," much more. 272pp. 5⅜ x 8¼. 0-486-27124-2

ARTS AND CRAFTS FURNITURE: The Complete Brooks Catalog of 1912, Brooks Manufacturing Co. Photos and detailed descriptions of more than 150 now very collectible furniture designs from the Arts and Crafts movement depict davenports, settees, buffets, desks, tables, chairs, bedsteads, dressers and more, all built of solid, quarter-sawed oak. Invaluable for students and enthusiasts of antiques, Americana and the decorative arts. 80pp. 6½ x 9¼. 0-486-27471-3

WILBUR AND ORVILLE: A Biography of the Wright Brothers, Fred Howard. Definitive, crisply written study tells the full story of the brothers' lives and work. A vividly written biography, unparalleled in scope and color, that also captures the spirit of an extraordinary era. 560pp. 6⅛ x 9¼. 0-486-40297-5

THE ARTS OF THE SAILOR: Knotting, Splicing and Ropework, Hervey Garrett Smith. Indispensable shipboard reference covers tools, basic knots and useful hitches; handsewing and canvas work, more. Over 100 illustrations. Delightful reading for sea lovers. 256pp. 5⅜ x 8½. 0-486-26440-8

FRANK LLOYD WRIGHT'S FALLINGWATER: The House and Its History, Second, Revised Edition, Donald Hoffmann. A total revision–both in text and illustrations–of the standard document on Fallingwater, the boldest, most personal architectural statement of Wright's mature years, updated with valuable new material from the recently opened Frank Lloyd Wright Archives. "Fascinating"–*The New York Times.* 116 illustrations. 128pp. 9¼ x 10¾. 0-486-27430-6

PHOTOGRAPHIC SKETCHBOOK OF THE CIVIL WAR, Alexander Gardner. 100 photos taken on field during the Civil War. Famous shots of Manassas Harper's Ferry, Lincoln, Richmond, slave pens, etc. 244pp. 10⅝ x 8¼. 0-486-22731-6

FIVE ACRES AND INDEPENDENCE, Maurice G. Kains. Great back-to-the-land classic explains basics of self-sufficient farming. The one book to get. 95 illustrations. 397pp. 5⅜ x 8½. 0-486-20974-1

CATALOG OF DOVER BOOKS

A MODERN HERBAL, Margaret Grieve. Much the fullest, most exact, most useful compilation of herbal material. Gigantic alphabetical encyclopedia, from aconite to zedoary, gives botanical information, medical properties, folklore, economic uses, much else. Indispensable to serious reader. 161 illustrations. 888pp. 6½ x 9¼. 2-vol. set. (Available in U.S. only.)   Vol. I: 0-486-22798-7   Vol. II: 0-486-22799-5

HIDDEN TREASURE MAZE BOOK, Dave Phillips. Solve 34 challenging mazes accompanied by heroic tales of adventure. Evil dragons, people-eating plants, bloodthirsty giants, many more dangerous adversaries lurk at every twist and turn. 34 mazes, stories, solutions. 48pp. 8¼ x 11.   0-486-24566-7

LETTERS OF W. A. MOZART, Wolfgang A. Mozart. Remarkable letters show bawdy wit, humor, imagination, musical insights, contemporary musical world; includes some letters from Leopold Mozart. 276pp. 5⅜ x 8½.   0-486-22859-2

BASIC PRINCIPLES OF CLASSICAL BALLET, Agrippina Vaganova. Great Russian theoretician, teacher explains methods for teaching classical ballet. 118 illustrations. 175pp. 5⅜ x 8½.   0-486-22036-2

THE JUMPING FROG, Mark Twain. Revenge edition. The original story of The Celebrated Jumping Frog of Calaveras County, a hapless French translation, and Twain's hilarious "retranslation" from the French. 12 illustrations. 66pp. 5⅜ x 8½.   0-486-22686-7

BEST REMEMBERED POEMS, Martin Gardner (ed.). The 126 poems in this superb collection of 19th- and 20th-century British and American verse range from Shelley's "To a Skylark" to the impassioned "Renascence" of Edna St. Vincent Millay and to Edward Lear's whimsical "The Owl and the Pussycat." 224pp. 5⅜ x 8½.   0-486-27165-X

COMPLETE SONNETS, William Shakespeare. Over 150 exquisite poems deal with love, friendship, the tyranny of time, beauty's evanescence, death and other themes in language of remarkable power, precision and beauty. Glossary of archaic terms. 80pp. 5³⁄₁₆ x 8¼.   0-486-26686-9

HISTORIC HOMES OF THE AMERICAN PRESIDENTS, Second, Revised Edition, Irvin Haas. A traveler's guide to American Presidential homes, most open to the public, depicting and describing homes occupied by every American President from George Washington to George Bush. With visiting hours, admission charges, travel routes. 175 photographs. Index. 160pp. 8¼ x 11.   0-486-26751-2

THE WIT AND HUMOR OF OSCAR WILDE, Alvin Redman (ed.). More than 1,000 ripostes, paradoxes, wisecracks: Work is the curse of the drinking classes; I can resist everything except temptation; etc. 258pp. 5⅜ x 8½.   0-486-20602-5

SHAKESPEARE LEXICON AND QUOTATION DICTIONARY, Alexander Schmidt. Full definitions, locations, shades of meaning in every word in plays and poems. More than 50,000 exact quotations. 1,485pp. 6½ x 9¼. 2-vol. set.
Vol. 1: 0-486-22726-X   Vol. 2: 0-486-22727-8

SELECTED POEMS, Emily Dickinson. Over 100 best-known, best-loved poems by one of America's foremost poets, reprinted from authoritative early editions. No comparable edition at this price. Index of first lines. 64pp. 5³⁄₁₆ x 8¼.   0-486-26466-1

THE INSIDIOUS DR. FU-MANCHU, Sax Rohmer. The first of the popular mystery series introduces a pair of English detectives to their archnemesis, the diabolical Dr. Fu-Manchu. Flavorful atmosphere, fast-paced action, and colorful characters enliven this classic of the genre. 208pp. 5³⁄₁₆ x 8¼.   0-486-29898-1

THE MALLEUS MALEFICARUM OF KRAMER AND SPRENGER, translated by Montague Summers. Full text of most important witchhunter's "bible," used by both Catholics and Protestants. 278pp. 6⅝ x 10. 0-486-22802-9

SPANISH STORIES/CUENTOS ESPAÑOLES: A Dual-Language Book, Angel Flores (ed.). Unique format offers 13 great stories in Spanish by Cervantes, Borges, others. Faithful English translations on facing pages. 352pp. 5⅜ x 8½.
0-486-25399-6

GARDEN CITY, LONG ISLAND, IN EARLY PHOTOGRAPHS, 1869–1919, Mildred H. Smith. Handsome treasury of 118 vintage pictures, accompanied by carefully researched captions, document the Garden City Hotel fire (1899), the Vanderbilt Cup Race (1908), the first airmail flight departing from the Nassau Boulevard Aerodrome (1911), and much more. 96pp. 8⅞ x 11¾. 0-486-40669-5

OLD QUEENS, N.Y., IN EARLY PHOTOGRAPHS, Vincent F. Seyfried and William Asadorian. Over 160 rare photographs of Maspeth, Jamaica, Jackson Heights, and other areas. Vintage views of DeWitt Clinton mansion, 1939 World's Fair and more. Captions. 192pp. 8⅞ x 11. 0-486-26358-4

CAPTURED BY THE INDIANS: 15 Firsthand Accounts, 1750-1870, Frederick Drimmer. Astounding true historical accounts of grisly torture, bloody conflicts, relentless pursuits, miraculous escapes and more, by people who lived to tell the tale. 384pp. 5⅜ x 8½. 0-486-24901-8

THE WORLD'S GREAT SPEECHES (Fourth Enlarged Edition), Lewis Copeland, Lawrence W. Lamm, and Stephen J. McKenna. Nearly 300 speeches provide public speakers with a wealth of updated quotes and inspiration—from Pericles' funeral oration and William Jennings Bryan's "Cross of Gold Speech" to Malcolm X's powerful words on the Black Revolution and Earl of Spenser's tribute to his sister, Diana, Princess of Wales. 944pp. 5⅜ x 8⅜. 0-486-40903-1

THE BOOK OF THE SWORD, Sir Richard F. Burton. Great Victorian scholar/adventurer's eloquent, erudite history of the "queen of weapons"—from prehistory to early Roman Empire. Evolution and development of early swords, variations (sabre, broadsword, cutlass, scimitar, etc.), much more. 336pp. 6⅛ x 9¼.
0-486-25434-8

AUTOBIOGRAPHY: The Story of My Experiments with Truth, Mohandas K. Gandhi. Boyhood, legal studies, purification, the growth of the Satyagraha (nonviolent protest) movement. Critical, inspiring work of the man responsible for the freedom of India. 480pp. 5⅜ x 8½. (Available in U.S. only.) 0-486-24593-4

CELTIC MYTHS AND LEGENDS, T. W. Rolleston. Masterful retelling of Irish and Welsh stories and tales. Cuchulain, King Arthur, Deirdre, the Grail, many more. First paperback edition. 58 full-page illustrations. 512pp. 5⅜ x 8½. 0-486-26507-2

THE PRINCIPLES OF PSYCHOLOGY, William James. Famous long course complete, unabridged. Stream of thought, time perception, memory, experimental methods; great work decades ahead of its time. 94 figures. 1,391pp. 5⅜ x 8½. 2-vol. set.
Vol. I: 0-486-20381-6   Vol. II: 0-486-20382-4

THE WORLD AS WILL AND REPRESENTATION, Arthur Schopenhauer. Definitive English translation of Schopenhauer's life work, correcting more than 1,000 errors, omissions in earlier translations. Translated by E. F. J. Payne. Total of 1,269pp. 5⅜ x 8½. 2-vol. set.   Vol. 1: 0-486-21761-2   Vol. 2: 0-486-21762-0

CATALOG OF DOVER BOOKS

MAGIC AND MYSTERY IN TIBET, Madame Alexandra David-Neel. Experiences among lamas, magicians, sages, sorcerers, Bonpa wizards. A true psychic discovery. 32 illustrations. 321pp. 5⅜ x 8½. (Available in U.S. only.) 0-486-22682-4

THE EGYPTIAN BOOK OF THE DEAD, E. A. Wallis Budge. Complete reproduction of Ani's papyrus, finest ever found. Full hieroglyphic text, interlinear transliteration, word-for-word translation, smooth translation. 533pp. 6½ x 9¼. 0-486-21866-X

HISTORIC COSTUME IN PICTURES, Braun & Schneider. Over 1,450 costumed figures in clearly detailed engravings–from dawn of civilization to end of 19th century. Captions. Many folk costumes. 256pp. 8⅜ x 11¾. 0-486-23150-X

MATHEMATICS FOR THE NONMATHEMATICIAN, Morris Kline. Detailed, college-level treatment of mathematics in cultural and historical context, with numerous exercises. Recommended Reading Lists. Tables. Numerous figures. 641pp. 5⅜ x 8½. 0-486-24823-2

PROBABILISTIC METHODS IN THE THEORY OF STRUCTURES, Isaac Elishakoff. Well-written introduction covers the elements of the theory of probability from two or more random variables, the reliability of such multivariable structures, the theory of random function, Monte Carlo methods of treating problems incapable of exact solution, and more. Examples. 502pp. 5⅜ x 8½. 0-486-40691-1

THE RIME OF THE ANCIENT MARINER, Gustave Doré, S. T. Coleridge. Doré's finest work; 34 plates capture moods, subtleties of poem. Flawless full-size reproductions printed on facing pages with authoritative text of poem. "Beautiful. Simply beautiful."–*Publisher's Weekly.* 77pp. 9¼ x 12. 0-486-22305-1

SCULPTURE: Principles and Practice, Louis Slobodkin. Step-by-step approach to clay, plaster, metals, stone; classical and modern. 253 drawings, photos. 255pp. 8⅛ x 11. 0-486-22960-2

THE INFLUENCE OF SEA POWER UPON HISTORY, 1660–1783, A. T. Mahan. Influential classic of naval history and tactics still used as text in war colleges. First paperback edition. 4 maps. 24 battle plans. 640pp. 5⅜ x 8½. 0-486-25509-3

THE STORY OF THE TITANIC AS TOLD BY ITS SURVIVORS, Jack Winocour (ed.). What it was really like. Panic, despair, shocking inefficiency, and a little heroism. More thrilling than any fictional account. 26 illustrations. 320pp. 5⅜ x 8½. 0-486-20610-6

ONE TWO THREE . . . INFINITY: Facts and Speculations of Science, George Gamow. Great physicist's fascinating, readable overview of contemporary science: number theory, relativity, fourth dimension, entropy, genes, atomic structure, much more. 128 illustrations. Index. 352pp. 5⅜ x 8½. 0-486-25664-2

DALÍ ON MODERN ART: The Cuckolds of Antiquated Modern Art, Salvador Dalí. Influential painter skewers modern art and its practitioners. Outrageous evaluations of Picasso, Cézanne, Turner, more. 15 renderings of paintings discussed. 44 calligraphic decorations by Dalí. 96pp. 5⅜ x 8½. (Available in U.S. only.) 0-486-29220-7

ANTIQUE PLAYING CARDS: A Pictorial History, Henry René D'Allemagne. Over 900 elaborate, decorative images from rare playing cards (14th–20th centuries): Bacchus, death, dancing dogs, hunting scenes, royal coats of arms, players cheating, much more. 96pp. 9¼ x 12¼. 0-486-29265-7

MAKING FURNITURE MASTERPIECES: 30 Projects with Measured Drawings, Franklin H. Gottshall. Step-by-step instructions, illustrations for constructing handsome, useful pieces, among them a Sheraton desk, Chippendale chair, Spanish desk, Queen Anne table and a William and Mary dressing mirror. 224pp. 8⅛ x 11¼. 0-486-29338-6

NORTH AMERICAN INDIAN DESIGNS FOR ARTISTS AND CRAFTSPEOPLE, Eva Wilson. Over 360 authentic copyright-free designs adapted from Navajo blankets, Hopi pottery, Sioux buffalo hides, more. Geometrics, symbolic figures, plant and animal motifs, etc. 128pp. 8⅜ x 11. (Not for sale in the United Kingdom.) 0-486-25341-4

THE FOSSIL BOOK: A Record of Prehistoric Life, Patricia V. Rich et al. Profusely illustrated definitive guide covers everything from single-celled organisms and dinosaurs to birds and mammals and the interplay between climate and man. Over 1,500 illustrations. 760pp. 7½ x 10⅛. 0-486-29371-8

VICTORIAN ARCHITECTURAL DETAILS: Designs for Over 700 Stairs, Mantels, Doors, Windows, Cornices, Porches, and Other Decorative Elements, A. J. Bicknell & Company. Everything from dormer windows and piazzas to balconies and gable ornaments. Also includes elevations and floor plans for handsome, private residences and commercial structures. 80pp. 9⅜ x 12¼. 0-486-44015-X

WESTERN ISLAMIC ARCHITECTURE: A Concise Introduction, John D. Hoag. Profusely illustrated critical appraisal compares and contrasts Islamic mosques and palaces–from Spain and Egypt to other areas in the Middle East. 139 illustrations. 128pp. 6 x 9. 0-486-43760-4

CHINESE ARCHITECTURE: A Pictorial History, Liang Ssu-ch'eng. More than 240 rare photographs and drawings depict temples, pagodas, tombs, bridges, and imperial palaces comprising much of China's architectural heritage. 152 halftones, 94 diagrams. 232pp. 10¾ x 9⅞. 0-486-43999-2

THE RENAISSANCE: Studies in Art and Poetry, Walter Pater. One of the most talked-about books of the 19th century, *The Renaissance* combines scholarship and philosophy in an innovative work of cultural criticism that examines the achievements of Botticelli, Leonardo, Michelangelo, and other artists. "The holy writ of beauty."–Oscar Wilde. 160pp. 5⅜ x 8½. 0-486-44025-7

A TREATISE ON PAINTING, Leonardo da Vinci. The great Renaissance artist's practical advice on drawing and painting techniques covers anatomy, perspective, composition, light and shadow, and color. A classic of art instruction, it features 48 drawings by Nicholas Poussin and Leon Battista Alberti. 192pp. 5⅜ x 8½. 0-486-44155-5

THE MIND OF LEONARDO DA VINCI, Edward McCurdy. More than just a biography, this classic study by a distinguished historian draws upon Leonardo's extensive writings to offer numerous demonstrations of the Renaissance master's achievements, not only in sculpture and painting, but also in music, engineering, and even experimental aviation. 384pp. 5⅜ x 8½. 0-486-44142-3

WASHINGTON IRVING'S RIP VAN WINKLE, Illustrated by Arthur Rackham. Lovely prints that established artist as a leading illustrator of the time and forever etched into the popular imagination a classic of Catskill lore. 51 full-color plates. 80pp. 8⅜ x 11. 0-486-44242-X

HENSCHE ON PAINTING, John W. Robichaux. Basic painting philosophy and methodology of a great teacher, as expounded in his famous classes and workshops on Cape Cod. 7 illustrations in color on covers. 80pp. 5⅜ x 8½. 0-486-43728-0

LIGHT AND SHADE: A Classic Approach to Three-Dimensional Drawing, Mrs. Mary P. Merrifield. Handy reference clearly demonstrates principles of light and shade by revealing effects of common daylight, sunshine, and candle or artificial light on geometrical solids. 13 plates. 64pp. 5⅜ x 8½.   0-486-44143-1

ASTROLOGY AND ASTRONOMY: A Pictorial Archive of Signs and Symbols, Ernst and Johanna Lehner. Treasure trove of stories, lore, and myth, accompanied by more than 300 rare illustrations of planets, the Milky Way, signs of the zodiac, comets, meteors, and other astronomical phenomena. 192pp. 8⅜ x 11.

0-486-43981-X

JEWELRY MAKING: Techniques for Metal, Tim McCreight. Easy-to-follow instructions and carefully executed illustrations describe tools and techniques, use of gems and enamels, wire inlay, casting, and other topics. 72 line illustrations and diagrams. 176pp. 8¼ x 10⅞.   0-486-44043-5

MAKING BIRDHOUSES: Easy and Advanced Projects, Gladstone Califf. Easy-to-follow instructions include diagrams for everything from a one-room house for bluebirds to a forty-two-room structure for purple martins. 56 plates; 4 figures. 80pp. 8¾ x 6⅜.   0-486-44183-0

LITTLE BOOK OF LOG CABINS: How to Build and Furnish Them, William S. Wicks. Handy how-to manual, with instructions and illustrations for building cabins in the Adirondack style, fireplaces, stairways, furniture, beamed ceilings, and more. 102 line drawings. 96pp. 8¾ x 6⅜.   0-486-44259-4

THE SEASONS OF AMERICA PAST, Eric Sloane. From "sugaring time" and strawberry picking to Indian summer and fall harvest, a whole year's activities described in charming prose and enhanced with 79 of the author's own illustrations. 160pp. 8¼ x 11.   0-486-44220-9

THE METROPOLIS OF TOMORROW, Hugh Ferriss. Generous, prophetic vision of the metropolis of the future, as perceived in 1929. Powerful illustrations of towering structures, wide avenues, and rooftop parks—all features in many of today's modern cities. 59 illustrations. 144pp. 8¼ x 11.   0-486-43727-2

THE PATH TO ROME, Hilaire Belloc. This 1902 memoir abounds in lively vignettes from a vanished time, recounting a pilgrimage on foot across the Alps and Apennines in order to "see all Europe which the Christian Faith has saved." 77 of the author's original line drawings complement his sparkling prose. 272pp. 5⅜ x 8½.

0-486-44001-X

THE HISTORY OF RASSELAS: Prince of Abissinia, Samuel Johnson. Distinguished English writer attacks eighteenth-century optimism and man's unrealistic estimates of what life has to offer. 112pp. 5⅜ x 8½.   0-486-44094-X

A VOYAGE TO ARCTURUS, David Lindsay. A brilliant flight of pure fancy, where wild creatures crowd the fantastic landscape and demented torturers dominate victims with their bizarre mental powers. 272pp. 5⅜ x 8½.   0-486-44198-9

Paperbound unless otherwise indicated. Available at your book dealer, online at **www.doverpublications.com**, or by writing to Dept. GI, Dover Publications, Inc., 31 East 2nd Street, Mineola, NY 11501. For current price information or for free catalogs (please indicate field of interest), write to Dover Publications or log on to **www.doverpublications.com** and see every Dover book in print. Dover publishes more than 500 books each year on science, elementary and advanced mathematics, biology, music, art, literary history, social sciences, and other areas.